THE

Also by Ian Strachan

THE
SECOND STEP

The sequel to
Journey of a Thousand Miles

Ian Strachan

MAMMOTH

First published in Great Britain 1991
by Methuen Children's Books Ltd
Published 1992 by Mammoth
an imprint of Reed Consumer Books Ltd
Michelin House, 81 Fulham Road, London SW3 6RB
and Auckland, Melbourne, Singapore and Toronto

Reprinted 1994

Copyright © 1991 Ian Strachan

ISBN 0 7497 0961 8

A CIP catalogue record for this title
is available from the British Library

Printed and bound in Great Britain
by Cox & Wyman Ltd, Reading, Berkshire

This book is dedicated to refugees all over the world who, for a variety of reasons and in increasing numbers, are forced to abandon their homes and seek a new life, and to the individuals and organisations which offer help when others turn their backs. These include UN High Commissioner for Refugees, the Red Cross, Red Crescent, Save the Children Fund and Ockenden Venture.

CONTENTS

'The journey of a thousand miles begins with one step.'

Lao-Tsze
The Simple Way

ONE

Lee, trying desperately to move casually, walked along the front of the featureless Admin Block. He paused as he reached the dumpy, red box that stood just inside the main gate and looked again at the letter in his hand. Once that letter, which explained exactly what he intended to try and do, was posted there could be no turning back. He would have committed himself to a plan of action and if he failed he couldn't believe he would ever be able to return and face his parents again.

His hand trembled slightly as he slipped the letter into the slit and heard it drop into the bottom of the box.

He refused to turn and check, certain that his furtive expression would give him away at once, but the prickling sensation in his neck convinced him that a thousand curious eyes were watching his every move. He just hoped that none of those eyes belonged to people who knew where he ought to be.

He'd chosen the middle of the morning because his family would all be occupied. Tam, his youngest sister, would be at her English class, Kim, the eldest, would probably be draped round some boy's neck, as usual! His parents should be on the other side of the camp, sitting with his grandmother, staring at the four blank, off-white walls of their living-quarters.

Lee knew he couldn't hang around all day. He must take the next few steps, the ones that would get him through the gate and on to the road to London.

The grey-haired English security guard, sitting in the office ready to lift the gate to admit vehicles, had already glanced twice in Lee's direction. Not that there was anything to stop Lee going out of the camp whenever he liked. The security man wasn't employed to keep the Vietnamese refugees in, but to control vehicles entering or leaving and to keep out cranks. These mostly came from the extreme right-wing British Movement who arrived, armed with racist placards to hurl abuse, or worse, at the inmates.

11

For Lee, the enormous difference on this occasion was that once outside the camp, unless he achieved his objective – to lift the hopes of his family from their lowest ebb ever – he had no intention of returning.

Two years confined behind the seemingly innocent trim beech hedge had turned out to be more than he could take. The fact that he was so full of doubt and insecurity about leaving, something which had grown like a canker inside him during the last year, proved to Lee how right he was to be going. The frustration and boredom inside the camp, the air of helplessness which seeped out of its very walls was beginning to sap his last drops of self-confidence. It was now or never!

Angered by his own indecisiveness, Lee strode forward, slipped off the edge of the pavement and banged his face on the upright metal post that supported the red and white striped lifting-gate.

Inside his office, the security man rose anxiously to his feet. 'Are you okay?'

The thickness of the glass window, the man's accent and Lee's feeling of stupidity at having drawn attention to himself meant the only word he caught was 'okay'. He grinned back foolishly at the man. 'Okay,' he called, waving a hand as if that proved that it were true, and kept on moving.

Even when he had passed the gate he couldn't relax. The road was not only busy, carrying speeding lorries and cars, but it was narrow, twisty with only a rough grass verge to walk on.

He pulled his thick, quilted anorak around him to keep out the cold, damp English wind. It was probably one of the most useful things his grandmother had ever pulled out of the mountain of secondhand clothing, that had confronted them on arrival at the camp.

The clothes had been generously donated by local people, but the majority were too thin, or too worn, to protect the Vietnamese, more used to semi-tropical weather, from the severity of the English winter. Nevertheless, there was something about being a refugee, having lost all one's possessions and with them a great deal of one's personality, which made one grab anything that came along. So they had begun their new life in England, shivering in ill-fitting clothing, until they were slowly able to acquire more appropriate sweaters and scarves.

As Lee stumbled along, keeping his head down against the back-draught from passing lorries, he could not help remembering the very first time he had travelled up this road.

Throughout the fifteen-hour flight from Hong Kong to the UK their spirits had been high from a heady mixture of freedom and anticipation but, finding themselves standing on the tarmac in the grey, damp dawn of Heathrow Airport, that mood had suddenly changed.

Herded together in a corner of the airport lounge, clutching their few belongings, white labels bearing their personal details tied to their outer clothing, they suddenly felt more like misdirected luggage than human beings.

Flustered, tall, pink English women had passed amongst them silently examining their labels and ticking names off on clipboards. The women spoke no Vietnamese, Lee had met very few westerners who did, and they appeared wholly unable to understand the halting English most of the Vietnamese had spent two years learning in the stuffy, corrugated-iron class-rooms back in Hong Kong. Like policewomen, they indicated by gestures which group of three the refugees should join.

When Tam had automatically attempted to follow her parents, without waiting to be officially checked off on their lists, one of the flustered women had abruptly pushed her back into line. Little Tam, convinced she was being permanently separated from her parents, promptly burst into tears.

Eventually they were all loaded on to the appropriate coaches. Tired and hungry, having eaten their last meal on the plane four hours previously, they were relieved when carrier bags of food and drink were handed to them as they boarded their coach. Relief turned to dismay when they looked inside the bags and realised the Englishwomen, out of a mixture of kindness and ignorance, had provided them with sandwiches, something they had seen but never eaten. Several people were so hungry that they tried, but found the curious thin squares of white bread, greasy butter and cold meat totally inedible. Which made them

13

doubly grateful for the fruit drinks that had been included.

Miserably they gazed out into the grey light at the unfamiliar landscape either side of the motorway. Like most people from abroad their knowledge of the UK was limited to pictures of Buckingham Palace and the Tower of London, they were unprepared for the bits in between.

Once the bus had left London, without seeing either of those two landmarks, and joined the motorway they seemed to pass through endless miles of fields of varying sizes, each bordered by hedges. Not remotely like the flat paddy fields with which most of them were familiar.

The houses, too, were strange. The Vietnamese were used to more crowded surroundings. Whole families, including grandparents, uncles and aunts, happily shared two- or three-roomed flats, which seemed to grow in piles like anthills. Here individual houses, often in their own grounds, were sometimes separated by these never-ending fields.

In complete silence they stared, red-eyed, at the alien landscape under its dull, grey shield of cloud. The laughter and chatter that had been so much part of the flight had disappeared completely and the only squeal of delight came from Tam.

From the night they had left Vietnam she'd been on a constant quest for dragons. She had mistaken the flames from the beacon, lit to attract rescuers to the deserted island on which they'd been stranded, for dragon's breath. Had watched wonderful dragons made from paper and silk dancing in the streets of Hong Kong during Chinese celebrations, but she had yet to encounter the real thing.

'Look, look! At last, a real dragon!' Tam cried out, pointing at a yellow tongue of flame that leaped and danced high into the leaden sky.

Everyone had laughed. Father had patiently explained that the flames were from an oil refinery where unwanted gases were being burned off, but Tam refused to believe him.

Only when they passed through Birmingham did they see anything like another city and by then they had a very distorted view of England as a deserted, green land with only minor pockets of building.

14

The coach journey lasted for nearly three hours before the bus left the motorway. Eventually it wound its way up the road Lee was walking down.

He remembered the anxious looks on the faces of his family as the bus had turned in through the gate and pulled up by the low, austere, creamy-coloured, main building.

Their brief period of freedom was over. They had left one transit camp back in Hong Kong only to find themselves in another. The only difference appeared to be that this one was bordered with hedges rather than high walls and barbed wire. It had yet to dawn on them that though hedges would only provide symbolic barriers, they would hold them far more securely than barbed wire ever had.

But at least there were other Vietnamese people already living here, who could explain what was going on.

'Where are the other two coaches that left the airport with us?' Lee's father asked the moment he'd clambered stiffly down the steps.

'They have probably gone to other camps,' a young Vietnamese man explained.

'Close by?'

The young man shook his head. 'Several hundred kilometres away.'

Slowly, the new arrivals realised that abruptly, with no farewells, families who had lived next to each other for two years and longer in Hong Kong and some, who came from the same village in Vietnam, had been separated. Best friends, neighbours, girlfriends and playmates had parted without knowing if they would ever meet again, or even be able to make contact with each other.

Partings and separation were something Lee had grown used to in the four years since he'd left Vietnam. Even within Lee's own family there was poor Uncle Loc, left behind in Hong Kong, and his grandfather who, having been such a tower of strength throughout the dangerous days of their voyage to freedom, had died within sight of Hong Kong.

And there were so many others.

Quan and his baby brother, both of whom had died in the South China Sea.

And of course, there was their sister, Chi.

Lee couldn't bring himself to think about Chi. The only thing which really worried Lee about walking out of this camp, apart from being separated from his parents, was that he might, at least for a while, lose contact with Chi. What if the letter he'd just posted to her, explaining everything, was to be his last? If he failed to achieve his objective that might be the price he'd have to pay.

To wipe out any lingering doubts, Lee stuffed his hands deep into his anorak pockets, bent his head into the biting cold wind and stumbled on along the grass verge.

He would have preferred to have left the main road, on which he felt very exposed, and gone cross-country but, from the previous journeys he'd made on foot and in the camp's minibus, Lee knew there was a road bridge he must use to cross a railway line.

He'd brought a few supplies. Tucked in the pockets of his anorak, were bars of chocolate, chewing gum, some cold chicken in a plastic bag, a couple of cartons of orange drink, things like that, but he'd been afraid to collect too much for fear of drawing attention to himself.

He had also remembered to bring matches, his black-handled clasp knife, originally a present from his grandfather, grandfather's fishing line and, of course, the two ten-pound notes.

That money had provided Lee with the opportunity to leave. It was so unusual, since he came to England, that he should have money that he'd seen it as a sign from the Gods. He had come by it in a curious way too.

TWO

The previous Sunday, Lee had been out for a walk. He was on his way back to the camp, thinking how cold, green and sunless England was, when he noticed a white car pulled in awkwardly on to the grass verge, with its bonnet up and a man fiddling with the engine.

Lee could read English perfectly well, given time, but he was very hesitant about speaking it. What few people he'd met outside the camp seemed difficult to understand because they mostly spoke in dialect. It embarrassed Lee to have to constantly ask them to repeat themselves, particularly when he still couldn't tell what they were saying.

He was about to hurry past when a tall, suntanned, blond man extricated himself from under the car bonnet and stood up. He neither stared at Lee, nor did he seem frightened, both reactions Lee was accustomed to when strangers found a Chinese-looking person wandering alone through the English countryside.

The man grinned at Lee. 'Hi!'

Lee found the man's smile infectious and grinned back. 'Hi.' Though Lee was positive he'd never met the man before, there was something oddly familiar about him.

'Know anything about cars?'

'Yes,' Lee said eagerly. He was already peering inside the engine before he realised the reason why he had no trouble understanding this man – he was American.

Lee had learned his first English back home in Vietnam from American servicemen. Also his father, who had worked in the Legal Department on a liaison project between the South Vietnamese and the Americans, spoke English with an American accent.

'What does your engine do?' Lee asked.

'That's the problem,' the man said cheerfully, 'it doesn't! It keeps cutting out on me. I put my foot on the gas and instead of going faster, it slows down. This time it stopped altogether.'

'Carburettor,' Lee suggested straight away. In his sixteen years he'd had a good deal of experience with engines of various sorts. In Vietnam, Lee had worked in backstreet garages on Saturday afternoons, secretly because his father had disapproved.

When they'd arrived in Hong Kong he'd got part-time work around the Sham Shui Po Transit Camp. By then Lee's father had dropped his objections. He had to admit that, during their perilous journey across the South China Sea, it had been partly due to Lee's skill with engines that they'd managed to reach Hong Kong at all.

'Tools?' Lee enquired.

'I don't know,' the American said, unlocking the boot. 'This isn't my car, I only hired it for the day to come and see my daughter, who lives around here. Hey, maybe you know her?'

'I don't think,' Lee murmured uncertainly. He knew very few English people apart from the volunteers and the local vicar, who came from the little village church to conduct services on Sunday mornings.

'Nancy Keever, works in your camp – you are Vietnamese, aren't you?'

'Oh, Nancy! Yes, I know Nancy.' No wonder the man had seemed familiar! The resemblance between father and daughter was obvious. Nancy had the same bright, friendly, blue eyes and the same smiling mouth full of strong, white teeth. They also both had straight, blond hair, though Nancy's was worn loose and hung halfway down her back.

Everybody in the camp knew Nancy, though sadly few of the present inmates had many dealings with her! She ran the Resettlement and Transport Offices. Being sent to see Nancy was a red-letter day, it meant you had a new home waiting for you outside and you were, at long last, able to leave the camp.

She also organised the rotas for the minibus, the only permanent form of transport the camp owned. Lee helped to maintain it and had often used the excuse of needing to order parts through Nancy to question her about life in America. Their brief chats, in a funny kind of way, often made him feel,

18

for a moment, a shade closer to Chi as he began to understand more of her adopted homeland.

'I'm Bill Keever.' The man held out his large hand.

Lee wiped the oil from his hand on the back of his jeans before shaking it. 'Lee Nguyen.'

From the boot, Bill produced a small, black plastic roll, tied with coarse ribbon, which he handed over to Lee. 'This feels as if it might be what you need.'

Lee opened the limited selection of tools, found what he needed to open up the carburettor and proceeded carefully to clean out the blocked jets. While he worked, Bill leaned against the bonnet chatting. 'How long have you been in the UK?'

'Two years.'

'Do you like it?'

Lee knew he must be polite, otherwise he would appear ungrateful. 'It is okay.'

'But not like home – how long since you left Vietnam?'

'Four years. We were two years in Hong Kong, too.'

'Did your family ... ' Bill broke off, ' ... you did come with your family?' Lee nodded. 'Did they choose to come to the UK?'

Lee shook his head. 'No, we wanted to go to the States, but they would not allow us.'

'Sorry about that.'

Lee stood back. 'You try your engine now?'

'Sure.'

Bill climbed into the car and turned the key. The engine instantly burst into life and he gave Lee a big thumbs up! 'You're a life-saver,' Bill called out of the window while Lee was shutting the bonnet.

'You are welcome,' Lee returned with a pleased grin.

'Get in then!' Bill said, as Lee made no move.

'It's not far, I can walk.'

'Nonsense! You've got to show me the way.'

Lee pointed. 'Straight down this road.'

'No, I meant where to look for Nancy inside the camp! Climb in.'

As they drove Bill probed Lee with a continual series of

questions ending up with, 'What do you do in your spare time, apart from mending cars?'

Lee shrugged. 'Not much.'

'You play any sports?'

'Tennis.'

Bill's eyes lit up. 'Really?'

'I started to play in Hong Kong and I play here too. I won two tournaments,' he added proudly.

'That's fantastic!'

'Not big ones,' Lee said quickly, thinking he might have exaggerated their importance.

Lee didn't explain that he'd chosen tennis rather than football largely by accident when he'd found a racket left in their hut at Sham Shui Po by one of the other refugees, though he'd quickly taken to the game. He not only enjoyed the opportunity for individual effort, the fiercely competitive quality of the game, but the practical side of Lee's character was fascinated by the variety of shot, speed and spin which he duly set about mastering.

Purely by luck he'd had a great deal of help in that direction while he was still in Sham Shui Po. He was having a haircut at Thieu's open-air barber's stall in the middle of the camp when he happened to mention playing tennis. The mechanical rhythm of the barber's scissors stopped.

'Did you know I once played in the French Open?' Thieu asked proudly. 'It was in the 'fifties, after the Japanese had left and Vietnam was still a French colony.'

Lee glanced at Thieu's reflection in the bamboo-framed mirror he'd lashed to a telegraph pole for the benefit of his customers. It was hard to see this quiet middle-aged man as a tennis ace!

'I haven't played for years but I've still got my racket and I could give you a few tips,' he offered.

Lee was half joking when he took up Thieu's offer but he'd been amazed at how much the man had been able to teach him. Other boys in the camp, seeing what they were doing, went out and bought rackets so that they could join in, until eventually the barber was running quite a school.

Not that there was a real court. They had to borrow part of the dusty, grassless soccer pitch in the centre of the camp. The lines were drawn out in the dust with the side of somebody's shoe and frequently got smudged by sliding feet which caused many heated arguments over whether a ball was in or out. They didn't even have a proper net but wove one, rather like making a hammock, from string which they suspended between the backs of two old chairs.

Nevertheless, despite the makeshift quality of the equipment, the games were always fiercely contested, though Lee usually came out victorious.

The school came to an abrupt end when the barber got accepted by the Australian immigration authorities. While all the other men and boys worried about who was going to cut their hair after Thieu left, Lee's only concern was losing his tennis coaching.

'Oh, you don't need me any more,' Thieu assured him. 'In eighteen months you've learned everything I know about the game. All you need now is to keep fit, plenty of jogging, and keep practising. Every day, mind!'

'I will, I promise.'

It was only after his arrival in England, when Lee briefly joined the camp soccer team and played in a couple of matches, that he discovered how fortunate he was to have chosen tennis as his main game.

The camp soccer team was taken out at least twice a week to play local teams, which was good in itself, but after the matches there were always social events, dictated by the type of team they played.

Grown-up matches usually ended up in public houses, with the men getting very drunk while the young players froze to death in the minibus. The socials after the matches organised by the church were, if anything, worse. At those they all stood about in dusty parish halls being offered the inevitable English sandwich, tea with milk in it and something pink and wobbly, that Lee thought was the most disgusting thing he'd ever tasted, which the English called blancmange! He knew they were only trying to be kind, but he was amazed that nobody seemed to

21

have the slightest notion of Vietnamese diet, even the basic fact that milk played almost no part in it.

But apart from the food, the English always wanted to talk! Lee was never confident enough to use his English and spent most of the time either grinning stupidly, or sitting silently in a corner.

Lee discovered that tennis held no such horrors and no language problems either. The score was all you needed to know. There were no social get-togethers after tennis tournaments, many of which were held at posh clubs that appeared to have only invited the Vietnamese as an afterthought and weren't too thrilled when Lee, or his friend Quoc, walked off with the trophy!

'Who do you play against in the camp?' Bill enquired.

'Nobody now,' Lee said sadly. 'I used to play with Quoc, but he left with his family three weeks ago and there is nobody else my age who is good enough.'

'Your game's got a bit rusty, I guess.'

'Please?'

'You're out of practice.'

Lee, guiltily remembering his promise to Thieu, nodded. For a while after Quoc had gone Lee used the side of a building to stay in practice, the only one with a flat concrete surround similar to a hard court. He'd drawn a net with chalk across the flat surface and practised there for hours. Though it was impossible to serve and difficult to attempt groundstrokes, there was plenty of opportunity for fast volleying. But that had been brought to a sudden end when the people who lived the other side of Lee's wall had complained about the incessant thump of the ball.

Bill pulled up at the main gate. The security man peered at them through the window, but when he saw Lee was one of the occupants of the car, he walked out and raised the pole that cut off the road without bothering to ask who Bill was.

Lee showed Bill how to drive round to Nancy's office, appropriately Block N. To reach it they passed the tennis courts, and as they were climbing out of the car Bill said, 'Give me half an hour with Nancy and we'll have a game of tennis.'

Lee was thrilled. 'You play?'

Bill grinned. 'Enough to always pack a racket whenever I come away.'

Lee raced along the tarmac path, across the rough grass and the narrow perimeter road, towards one of a line of cream-painted, single-storey brick buildings each with a bright red roof. They were all identical. Several times Lee had run into the wrong block.

The camp had been built during World War II to house munitions workers and after that it had briefly housed an overflow of students from a nearby teacher's training college, until they had protested at the squalid conditions. Following their departure it had lain, dilapidated and empty for quite a while, until the County Council had responded to an urgent appeal from the British government to take a large number of Vietnamese Boat People who had been rescued at sea off a ship called the *Sibonga*.

The imminent arrival of two hundred people had prevented any but the most superficial repairs and although the place was clean, the staff fought a constant battle as doors fell off hinges, water systems leaked and, worst of all for the Vietnamese unused to England's low temperatures, the antiquated central heating system regularly went on the blink, or broke down completely.

Almost all the original two hundred refugees had left quite quickly, only to be replaced by a constant stream of new arrivals, who tended to stay longer and the staff were kept too busy tackling everyday repairs to contemplate serious renovation work, even if they had had the funds.

The Nguyen family lived in a block which bore the big letter C, painted in black on a white square. Here, the six of them occupied three rooms, each about seven feet square. The partitions between the rooms were very thin and, night or day, the slightest noise carried through them. There were dark, cold communal bathrooms at either end of the block, with showers and taps which dripped into chipped white sinks.

Lee shot through the bluey-grey outer door into the dimly-lit, echoing corridor, which ran through the centre of the building, and turned off into the first room on the left.

His parents sat on one bed, his grandmother sat opposite them. This was how they spent most days, staring at each other or the blank walls, apart from regular trips to the dining-room, attending lectures, or occasional visits to the library.

Sometimes they talked, but more often they spent hour after hour in complete silence, lost in their own thoughts, most of which were about their homeland, projecting images of people and places they'd known in Vietnam on to the blank white walls.

'Lee, where've you been?' his mother asked.

'Out for a walk. Have you seen my tennis racket?'

'Tennis racket? No, of course I haven't. If it's anywhere it'll be in your room.'

As Lee moved out into the corridor he collided with a woman, who'd only recently arrived in the camp, carrying a baby. 'I'm sorry,' he said, but the woman didn't seem to notice him. The baby was teething and keeping everybody in the block awake, including the mother, who looked tired and drawn.

Lee was lucky. Out of the whole family he was the only one who didn't have to share. His parents and grandmother shared one room, his sisters had another. Kim resented it, believing she was far too old to have to share with her little sister.

'It's either that,' Father decided, 'or Kim can come in with us and you share with your grandmother.'

Knowing her grandmother bitterly disapproved of almost everything she did, from her use of make-up to relationships with boys, Kim had chosen the lesser evil!

Lee's room, sandwiched between the other two, contained an iron-framed bed, a dull painted wardrobe, a small scratched table and a rickety upright chair. The only bright note was a piece of old red carpet in the centre of the floor, its curled-up edges revealing the dusty concrete floor beneath.

He searched under the bed and then rooted round in the bottom of the wardrobe amongst the cardboard boxes, shoes and clean shirts.

His racket was right at the back.

Next door he heard his grandmother, who was going deaf, shouting, 'What does he want?'

'His racket,' Mother explained.

'His what?' the old lady demanded loudly.

'HIS TENNIS RACKET!' Mother shouted back.

Lee sighed as he continued the search, this time for a ball. Even when they weren't really having a row they spent all their time shouting at each other.

'Mum, where's my tennis ball?' Lee shouted through the wall.

'Has he found his racket?' Grandmother interrupted.

'He's looking for a ball now.'

'What?'

'HE'S LOOKING FOR A BALL!'

'A wall?'

'NO, A BALL!'

If it wasn't so tragic, Lee thought, it would be funny. Being the oldest family member Grandmother, in keeping with tradition, had taken over the role as its leader following Grandfather's death. But with her non-existent English she was unable to conduct family affairs with outsiders except through an interpreter and, as her deafness grew worse, only one who spoke very clearly and loudly. Conscious of her declining status, she was apt to get very angry and frustrated, though the family tried to ease her situation by consulting her whenever possible.

Lee tried again. 'Have you seen it anywhere?'

Lee's father appeared in the doorway looking angry. 'Don't shout at your mother like that, have you no respect? You want to talk to us, you come into our room.'

'The walls are so thin there's no need,' Lee pointed out reasonably.

'Don't be insolent!' his father snapped back. 'We don't want everyone in the block listening to our business.'

'I only want a tennis ball. It's hardly a state secret!'

For a moment Lee's father looked as if he was about to hit Lee. He didn't, but in those few seconds Lee couldn't help remembering the quiet, confident, smiling man his father had once been. Now he was pale, he stooped slightly, his face was lined and his hair was going prematurely grey.

'I'm sorry, Father,' Lee said quickly and squeezed past him

to go next door to his mother. 'Please, have you seen my ball anywhere?'

'I think Tam was playing with it,' she said quietly, 'try her room.'

As Lee went back down the corridor he passed his father, still framed by Lee's doorway.

Lee pushed open the girls' door to find Kim doing her hair.

'Don't you ever knock?' she demanded indignantly.

'Sorry! Have you seen my tennis ball.'

'Of course not – what would I want with that?'

'Tam had it.'

'Oh, Tam!' Kim said scornfully. 'If you can find it you're welcome to it!' she added and gestured towards Tam's half of the room.

It looked as if a giant had grabbed all Tam's belongings, toys, sweet wrappers, empty fruit juice boxes, clothes and bedclothes, and had tossed them up in the air, letting them fall where they would.

By contrast Kim's side was neat and tidy, the bed made and all her clothes stored neatly in the wardrobe. Kim had a table, like Lee's, but hers, with the help of a bamboo place mat and an old mirror rescued from a rubbish skip, had transformed it into a dressing-table.

During his search through Tam's jumble Lee came across the doll he'd promised to buy Tam during the voyage when she'd realised that all hers had been left at home. It was one of the first things he'd bought with his earnings from his job at the Kowloon garage.

He'd been on his way to work when he first spotted the big doll on a street stall. She had long auburn hair, which could be washed and set, and was dressed in bright blue. When he'd returned to the camp carrying the doll, Tam thought it was the most wonderful thing she'd ever owned and she'd played with it for hours. She called her Suzie, after an American girl she'd known, and couldn't get to sleep without her. Suzie came to meals, family discussions and if, occasionally, she got mislaid, the whole family would have to search for her.

Now the doll had a leg missing, one of the eyes wouldn't close properly and the blue dress was grubby and torn.

But underneath Suzie he found his tennis ball! He glanced at his digital watch. Had he taken too long – was he late? He ran out into the corridor.

'Shut the door!' Kim shouted after him.

He raced past his father, still gazing vacantly into space and his mother, who called after him. 'Don't forget we eat in half an hour.'

'What?' his grandmother screamed.

By the time his mother had repeated the information, Lee had passed through the outer door and was on his way to the tennis courts.

THREE

Bill stood framed by the court's wire-netting gateway. The well-defined muscles on his tanned arms and legs contrasted with his white shorts and shirt. He wore Nike tennis shoes and gripped one of the latest lightweight, metal-framed rackets. A net of new, yellow tennis balls hung from his wrist.

As Lee walked out on to the red shale of the court he suddenly felt very silly. He'd got carried away by his enthusiasm at the possibility of a game after so long but it was clear that Bill Keever was in very good shape. Lee couldn't help wondering if he was out of his depth.

He felt shabby, too. He had got some ill-fitting, yellowing tennis shorts he'd pulled out from the bottom of the camp's clothing pile and worn for tournaments but, apart from finding them very chilly, it had never crossed his mind that Bill would bother to change for what had sounded more like a knockabout. Lee was wearing an old pair of jeans and a tee-shirt. His wooden racket was old, the tension in the strings was suspect and the muddy-grey ball he'd spent so long searching for was balding.

The chain-link fence which surrounded the court always reminded him of the fence round Sham Shui Po Transit Camp and as Bill pulled the gate to with a noisy clang Lee began to feel more confined than usual.

But Bill seemed to notice none of these things. 'I thought you'd changed your mind and weren't coming,' he grinned. 'Nancy tells me she's seen you playing and you're pretty good.' Lee didn't say anything, he just shuffled his feet uncomfortably. 'How about we have a little bet on this game? I've got ten pounds that says I can beat you in three sets.'

Lee no longer doubted him. 'But if I lose I could not pay you!' Lee protested. 'I have no money.'

He felt ashamed. They hadn't been so poor in Hong Kong. Most people in the Sham Shui Po Transit Camp who wanted work had found it. Kim had had a full-time job in a factory cutting out jeans. Mother, Grandmother and even Tam had earned money by sitting on their bunks all day assembling plastic parts into toys. Father's knowledge of Vietnamese law had not been much use in Hong Kong, but other refugees, many of whom could not even read or write Vietnamese and who certainly couldn't understand written English, were happy to pay him to write letters home for them and fill in the continuous pile of forms and all-important immigration applications.

The money they had earned helped them to retain their sense of self-respect, something they had lost entirely since coming to England. They had not come seeking charity, which was how they regarded the money they got from the DHSS. They had come prepared to work hard to build a new life. But they arrived at a time when there were already three million unemployed in the UK and the Vietnamese, with little English, had to get in line at the end of the queue. On top of this their camp was six miles from the nearest town, in the heart of the country, where the likelihood of their finding work was nil.

Lee knew all he had in his pocket was the change from a pound left over from some pocket money his father had grudgingly given him a month ago.

Bill seemed unaware of Lee's reaction. 'I haven't paid you yet for repairing my car.' He handed Lee a crisp, ten-pound note. 'That can be your stake.'

'Please?'

'Now, you can bet your ten against mine. Let's get on with the game.'

The silver dollar Bill tossed into the air to determine serve glinted meanly like a sly wink in the afternoon sunlight. Lee called and lost. Bill sent down a gentle ball which Lee drove back over the net with a strong forehand.

'Oh,' Bill called out, 'so that's the way it's going to be!'

Though Lee understood the words, he failed to catch the tone of sarcasm behind Bill's remark and thought his punishing return had offended the man in some way. Maybe, despite all his stunning kit, the man wasn't so hot after all. Perhaps he should have shown more consideration for the man's age, not hit the ball so hard and like his father had said only a few moments earlier, shown some respect. After all, it wasn't really *his* money. Lee could afford to lose the match and the bet without losing face.

Lee didn't feel very good about the game anyway and by now he didn't care if he won or not. He restrained his play, kept his shots weaker and instead of running for difficult balls let them go. The first set was soon over. Bill won 6 – 1.

So he was rather surprised, as they crossed beside the net post, when Bill stopped him by putting a hand on his shoulder. 'Something tells me you're not giving this your best shot.'

'Please?'

'You aren't playing your best, for some reason.'

Nancy, who'd wandered down to the court to watch and lay stretched out on the grass, cut in, 'I've never seen Lee play so badly. He used to be so aggressive.'

Bill fixed Lee with a serious look. 'If you think you're doing me a favour letting me win, then forget it! To be honest, I'd just as soon not play at all as keep going like this.'

After that Lee held nothing back. When he sped across the court and returned a particularly difficult ball his feeling for the game, which had begun to evaporate after Quoc left, began to return and with it his old competitive spirit, something Lee thought he'd lost for good.

As his touch improved, Lee felt the blood coursing through his veins for the first time in months and the hours of tuition he'd received from Thieu back in Hong Kong were really paying off.

Bill was quick to notice the sudden improvement. He grinned acknowledgement of a neat backhand pass Lee placed right in the corner, just inside the base line.

After his next serve Bill ran in to the net to volley Lee but Lee calmly changed the pace and sent a top spin lob way above Bill's outstretched racket. The ball dropped right on the line like a dead thing before Bill could get near it and Nancy applauded enthusiastically.

Lee, knowing he was playing well, felt his true personality returning. Gone was the drab, grey, lifeless refugee who mooched about the camp day after day. His brain, in tune with his body, had quicksilver reactions and split-second timing again.

But although Lee's game had improved beyond belief, the better his play became the stronger Bill's game got too and Lee, sensing the battle he had on his hands, now relished the taste of it.

Very slowly, Lee started to gain towards the end of the second set. The crunch came when Lee took Bill's service game. Despite being taken to deuce and three set points, Lee won with a superb smash, so powerful that the ball firmly wedged itself in the wire mesh at the back of the court and Lee held his own serve to take the set.

'This is more like it! One set each and everything to play for,' Bill said enthusiastically, towelling himself off before changing ends.

Lee merely grinned. The opponents he'd beaten in the tournaments had been around his own age and, though a little taller, they were evenly matched in terms of skill and strength. Theoretically Bill was completely out of his class, yet Lee realised he was more than holding his own. He knew he was involved in the most challenging match he'd ever played and somehow he sensed, though he couldn't explain why, that the result would affect far more than whether he won ten pounds or not.

In the third set they both gave it everything they'd got. Bill, despite his fitness was red-faced and Lee could feel the sweat pouring off him as he maintained the pace and speed.

Any advantage Bill might have had over him in height or strength, Lee more than made up for in speed around the court. Not only did he keep reaching impossible balls as Bill swung the ball from one side of the court to the other, but he managed to control his returns too, sending them zinging down, just inside the lines, to score point after point.

Lee won the final set 6 – 0 and Bill, hot and breathing hard, willingly handed over another ten-pound note. 'You're a great player, I haven't enjoyed a match that much in years.' He turned to his daughter. 'Is there somewhere we can get a drink? – I'm pooped!'

Nancy led the way into the main building to a room where a

table had been placed across the doorway to form the counter of a shop. She bought them both cartons of orange juice which they took back to her office.

While they were drinking Bill questioned Lee deeply about the journey he'd made from Vietnam to Hong Kong. That was a taboo subject amongst the Vietnamese. It was like the unspoken rule in jail that prisoners should not ask each other about the crime which had brought them there. They had to wait until the information was offered.

For the Vietnamese, many of whom had lost relatives in horrific circumstances, the experience, even if it had taken place several years ago, was regarded as very personal and too traumatic to be the subject of idle conversation.

But Lee felt differently. Compared to his life in England he regarded the voyage as a high point, after all he would never otherwise have met Chi. For him it had been an amazing adventure and one he never tired of reliving.

Besides which he found Bill Keever unusually easy to talk to and very well-informed on the subject of Vietnam and the plight of the Boat People. His contribution to the conversation went beyond simple, polite murmurs of sympathy to carefully-considered observations on what might be done to help the people who had already left and maybe removing the need for people to leave their homeland in the first place.

Because there was no lack of understanding of the kind that had left Lee struck dumb at vicarage teas, he told the whole story, missing out none of the people on board, or their joys and tragedies.

When his story was done one thing still puzzled Bill. 'So how come you and your family couldn't get into the States?'

'I don't know. My father worked for the Americans in Saigon. In Hong Kong he filled in many forms, but every time we were turned down.'

Bill Keever looked thoughtful, but soon after he checked his watch and stood up to leave. 'Lee, you'll have to excuse me. I guess I'd better shower and change. I'm taking my beautiful daughter out for a meal and then I've got to drive back to London.'

33

'To get a plane back to America?' Lee asked wistfully, thinking how wonderful it would be if he could do that.

'At the end of the week. I'm over here for an international conference that's being held in London's Albert Hall and I fly back on Friday night, right after the end of the conference. I've come here from a three-week fact-finding trip to the Gulf and before that I was in Brussels for a fortnight, so I shall be glad to get back home,' he admitted.

'Where is your home?' Lee asked.

'I don't spend much time there, but it's San Francisco.'

Lee's heart jumped, but he turned on Nancy and said accusingly, 'You never told me you lived in San Francisco.'

'You never asked me,' Nancy said with a smile.

Lee swung back to Bill. 'I wish I could go with you.'

Bill was intrigued. 'San Francisco particularly?'

Lee nodded. 'I have a friend living there.'

'Would that be Chi, the girl you kept mentioning when you were telling me about the boat journey?'

Lee nodded slowly. It was nearly two and a half years since they'd parted. But even now, when he remembered her climbing into the truck with her family, ready to leave Sham Shui Po for the airport, he felt tears welling up in his eyes.

'Excuse me, please,' he said abruptly. 'I have to go now, my family are waiting.'

'Hey, wait up a minute … ' Bill said, but Lee was already through the door and running away up the track.

FOUR

Lee ran blindly through the camp, pushing his body and sucking in air, until the tiredness from the physical effort of the tennis match was slowly supplanted by the muscular pain of his sprint over the rough ground.

As he ran Lee forced his mind to concentrate on each individual step in an attempt to erase the disturbing images of Chi which Bill had brought into his mind.

'Better you forget,' his mother had urged, the night Chi had left, as they stood in the drizzle watching families climbing into the truck which would take them to the airport and the start of their new life in America. 'Remembering will only cause you pain.'

He *had* tried to forget, but when he least expected it, startlingly clear pictures of Chi would spring unsummmoned into his mind. Pictures of them sitting side by side in the dark on the boat's engine-house roof, shyly exchanging words other than the ones they really wanted to say. Of Chi, gathering firewood on the deserted island where they were stranded, delighted to have her feet on dry land and actually fearing rescue because that would mean her being forced to go back on the very sea that had already claimed the lives of her two younger brothers.

But the most disturbing picture, a simple one, yet one which turned up in Lee's head with unsettling regularity, was of Chi squatting on the ground on the edge of Sham Shui Po camp. Behind her were the square holes of the chain-link fence segmenting the view of Hong Kong harbour. She wore traditional black trousers with a brown sweater. In front of her was a red plastic bowl and she patiently washed her family's rice bowls, as she did several times a day.

Lee couldn't understand why that simple action, repeated time after time in his mind, tore at his heart, but he ran faster and faster to try and rid himself of it.

Only when the image was obliterated did Lee eventually jog

across to the main building, by then bursting to pass on to his parents the good news about his tennis triumph over the American.

In the dining-hall most of the long wooden tables and benches, outdated equipment rescued from a school before it was sent for scrap, were empty. Lee was late, most of the diners had eaten and left. There were a group of North Vietnamese fishermen sitting smoking at one table, a mother and three young children at another, and Lee's family in the far corner.

'You're late!' his father said crossly.

'Sorry, I told you I was going to play tennis and guess what?'

'What?' asked Tam who was playing a complicated version of cat's cradle with Kim.

'I won! Two sets to one.'

'Who were you playing?' Kim asked, one hand absent-mindedly combing through her long black hair with her delicate fingers before she carefully took the threads Tam was offering her.

'You know Nancy in the Resettlement Office?'

At the mention of her name Father paid attention. 'The American girl? You played her?'

'Not her, her father! He's over here for a conference and he came to see Nancy.'

Father's expression grew very stern. 'And you wasted your time playing tennis with him?'

Too full of his success to notice the restrained anger in his father's voice, Lee rattled on. 'He was very good, but I still managed to beat him.'

'How could you be so stupid?' his father demanded.

Lee stopped dead. 'What do you mean?'

'Do you not remember how hard we tried to get to America?' Lee nodded. 'And why weren't we allowed to go?'

'I don't know, you never told us. You kept saying I was too young to understand.'

'There were several reasons why they rejected us, but the main one was that we had no sponsor. Everyone who goes to the States must have someone already living there, to sign a piece of paper saying they will help the family when they have arrived.

36

The Duongs had an uncle, already a naturalised citizen, who acted as their sponsor. You have just spent hours in the company of an American whom you could have introduced to your family. Don't you see? I could have asked *him* to sponsor us. Instead you not only waste time playing a stupid game of tennis with him, you make him lose face by beating him!'

In the silence which followed Father's tirade, Tam dropped the threads of the cradle and shuffled nervously along the bench, sidling into her mother's arms. Lee gazed miserably at the bare planks of the table. As Kim wound up the thread they'd been playing with the light glinted off the silver nail varnish on her carefully manicured, long nails.

It caught Father's eye. 'How many times have I told you about using nail varnish? I will not have my daughter going around looking like a Saigon bar girl!'

Kim burst into tears and ran out of the dining-hall.

'I'm sorry,' Lee said quietly. 'Maybe he's still somewhere around with Nancy. I could go and ask him.'

'How, when you have shamed him?'

'We could still ask Nancy to sponsor us? She's American too,' Lee said brightly.

Father couldn't believe his son's stupidity. 'And don't you think everybody in the camp has thought of that idea? There is just one obstacle, Nancy lives here, not in America! A sponsor has to be a resident!'

'I hadn't thought of that.'

'No,' Father said forcibly. 'You waste your life messing with car engines and playing tennis, why should you think about your family's future when you don't even worry about your own? It's time you thought about getting some qualifications towards a profession.'

Mother intervened. 'Leave the boy now,' she urged. 'You've made your point and Lee understands what he's done wrong. Let him eat.'

Though Grandmother, whose hearing came and went at the most inconvenient times, didn't catch the words, she was shocked by the tone of rebuke Mother had adopted. 'How dare you speak to my son in that way? You should know your place.

37

It is no wonder your children are out of control and have no respect for their elders.'

As the disagreement turned into a full-scale argument, Lee slid off the bench and made his way to the kitchen hatch. The air was steamy with washing-up.

'Is there any food left?' Lee called out.

Trinh looked over his shoulder. He'd been the masterly skipper of the boat which had taken them to Hong Kong and now, whenever Lee saw him in the humble role of cook, it underlined the level to which they had all sunk in their fruitless search for a better life. Not that the status of Trinh's job ever seemed to bother him and at least he *had* a job!

'You've left it late this time, young one!' Trinh said with a grin. Trinh and Lee, together with Lee's grandfather had been very close during the voyage and that bond between them had not weakened. 'I think I can find you something, though it may not be very hot.'

'I don't mind.'

Trinh brought him a bowl of rice topped with a little chicken and green vegetables. Lee got out his chopsticks and ate hungrily.

Trinh leant against the counter watching him. 'What's up, you're very quiet tonight?'

Lee sighed. 'They're all arguing again.'

Trinh nodded. 'This waiting, it gets to us all. Never mind, one day it will be over. Nancy will call for you to tell you they've found you a house and you'll be able to leave this place.'

'That seems less likely every day.'

'I know it takes a time, but believe me, you stand more chance than I do! Me, a single man! They'll never find a place for me. At least you're a family, that counts for more.'

'We *were* a family,' Lee corrected. 'Now we fight all day long, usually about the stupidest things. Like whether Kim should wear high-heeled shoes, or who should have the bathroom first! Sometimes I wish we'd never left home!'

'Hey, now, wait a minute!' Trinh held up a hand. 'Don't forget the problems we ethnic Chinese had back home. No jobs, no food, the secret police on our backs all the time. This camp may not be where we'd choose to live, but at least we have a roof over our heads, I cook you good meals and there are no secret police.' Trinh spread his arms wide. 'And you don't *have* to stay, nothing keeps you here! Remember what they said the first day we arrived? We aren't prisoners here. We can walk out any time we like. The only reason they recommended that we stay was because they think they might find the best opportunities for us. But there's nothing to stop us walking out of the front gate and taking on the world ourselves. Me – I don't have that kind of courage!'

When Lee thought about his brief accompanied trips in the minibus to the nearest town, or the supervised visits to places of interest, he had to admit he wasn't that brave either. If it hadn't been for the English volunteers who'd gone with them the simplest things would have defeated them.

On their first shopping trip they had been dismayed to arrive in town to find the shops all closed.

'Why bring us shopping when there are no shops open?' everyone had demanded.

The Englishman had smiled. 'They *are* open.'

'The doors are shut, how can they be open?'

In Vietnam, and even in Hong Kong, a shop open for trade kept its door wide open, but in England most shop doors stay closed.

'It's because of our climate,' the Englishman explained, 'but if you want to go in to buy something, you simply push the door open.'

'But with the door shut,' the Vietnamese pointed out, 'you cannot see what the shopkeeper looks like. He might be a crook and you wouldn't want to go in his shop.'

If simple things like that defeat us, Lee thought, how could we ever cope alone in this foreign country?

Yet, after he'd left the dining-hall and was wandering around the building, Trinh's words and the idea of leaving, kept rattling around in his mind. Probably because that simple thought had never occurred to him before. Maybe he could even go in search of Chi?

Lee laughed at himself for having such an outlandish idea and went into the recreation hall to play table tennis but his mind wasn't really on the game. It only served to remind him of beating Bill Keever and the telling off he'd received for his pains.

Feeling restless, and to give his father time to calm down, Lee wandered aimlessly from block to block, catching conversations with whoever he happened to meet.

As he was passing through J Block he came upon Tran Van Tuyen. Tran, who sported a crew cut, was more adventurous than most. He'd only just returned from visiting some friends who'd been rehoused in London. He was sitting on a bed in Lo's room telling him all the news. Lee stood in the doorway listening.

'They've got this flat on the sixteenth floor of a tower block,' Tran was explaining.

'Lucky people,' Lo said.

'Not so lucky!' Tran said. 'They've had a lot of trouble with the neighbours.'

'Trouble?'

'Some people put 'Keep Britain Pure' stickers on their front door and they've been spat on in the street. They even had to board up their letter box when someone started pushing lighted newspapers and packages of excrement through it.'

'It's not the first time that's happened,' Lo murmured grimly.

'If they didn't want us here, why did they invite us to come?' Lee asked bitterly.

The two older boys glanced up. 'It's just a stupid fringe element,' Tran said. 'Most people just leave us to get on with our own lives, which is all we want.'

They discussed their relationships with the English for a while before Tran completely changed the subject. 'I met these two guys, a bit older than me. They're part of a six-man co-operative who've opened a Vietnamese restaurant in Swiss Cottage, that's North London,' Tran said airily, 'and they're doing very well.'

'Like the co-op in Birmingham and the other one in Wales where they make jewellery,' Lo suggested.

'Exactly. It's the obvious way, isn't it? With so many unemployed English people we've got to make chances for ourselves,' Tran said.

'Which only works,' Lee pointed out, 'for the people who've got some gold left to use as capital. That excludes most of us, particularly anyone who got robbed by the pirates.'

Tran remembered some more news. 'Something else I found out from those two men; the Morning Star Battalion is growing.'

Lee had never heard of them before. 'Who are they – some sort of army?'

'That's right,' said Lo. 'It's an offshoot of the Overseas Volunteer Forces for the Restoration of Vietnam.'

'An underground branch,' Tran added, 'that supports President Nguyen Van Thiu.'

Lee had seen recent photographs of the exiled Vietnamese president standing outside a huge mock-Tudor mansion in Wimbledon. Until then he'd only thought of Wimbledon in connection with the tennis championships. That house was so far outside Lee's experience of anything that anybody could possibly live in, that he took it to be some sort of presidential castle. 'What's the Battalion hoping to do?'

'They're looking for young volunteers,' Tran said.

Lee still didn't understand. 'But to do what?'

'They've got a lot of rich businessmen in France and America involved with the movement who'd be willing to pay for anyone to go back to Vietnam as an undercover guerrilla and do sabotage to de-stabilise the North Vietnamese government.'

'But the Vietnamese wouldn't let them in,' Lee protested. 'You couldn't arrive at the airport and say, "I've decided to come back to do some sabotage!"'

Later that night as he lay on his bed he couldn't help thinking that the objectives of the Morning Star Battalion were more than a little ambitious. Though most Vietnamese, no matter how settled they had become abroad, would give anything to return home, he couldn't believe that what the entire might of the US army had failed to achieve could be accomplished by a handful of volunteers with a few sticks of gelignite. But he had to admire their idealism and idiotic though the idea sounded, anything, he thought, might be better than the present atmosphere of aimlessness and constant bickering over trifles. Except, the thought of returning to Vietnam without Chi was something he knew he couldn't do.

Even so, when he fell asleep his dreams were of once more walking the streets of Saigon, or Ho Chi Minh City as it was now called, though this time in the guise of an enemy agent!

At midnight Lee's alarm, and a number of others around the camp, went off. He switched on the short wave radio he'd bought in Hong Kong with part of his garage wages.

Every day the refugees tuned in to the Vietnamese news broadcasts not only of the BBC, but also from the Voice of America and the less reliable Radio Hanoi.

The familiar tones of the BBC World Service broadcasting to Vietnam filled his cold English room. Listening to reports of familiar places, read in his own language, Lee was filled, as always, with a deep feeling of homesickness.

Amongst the usual stories of rice crop failures and troubles on the Cambodian border between the Vietnamese army and the Khmer Rouge, Lee's attention was particularly taken by news of an explosion which had destroyed a bridge and severed the all-important rail link along the coast between North and South Vietnam.

When he'd switched off the radio after the fifteen-minute broadcast, Lee couldn't help wondering if that explosion had been the work of the Morning Star Battalion? Perhaps it wasn't such a silly idea after all.

When he went back to sleep he suffered again his worst recurring nightmare. He was watching their escape boat at the moment the pirates' junk had come alongside and the events were so far following the true story. Lee was perched on the gunnel of the junk. The pirates were completing their search for gold aboard the refugee boat. They searched Khai, found the gold concealed in the heel of his shoe and then carelessly tossed him overboard to drown while his wife screamed and screamed.

Then reality got sharply bent into fiction, as the pirates discovered Chi hidden beneath the deck.

42

Lee was forced to watch, powerless, as they hauled her out, crying, her clothes stinking with bilge-water. As the pirates dragged the terrified, helpless Chi across to the pirate ship, the fattest of the pirates made Lee, just as he had on that awful day, jump back to his own ship.

From there Lee had no choice, but to stand on his boat's engine-house roof, watching the departing pirate junk and listening to Chi's desperate cries for help gradually fading into the distance as they carried her off.

Lee woke violently. The light was on and his mother knelt beside the bed, stroking his forehead, wiping away the cold sweat of fear. 'Your nightmare again?' she asked gently.

'Did I scream out?'

She nodded.

'I'm sorry, I didn't mean to wake everybody,' he said, embarrassed by the tears that were streaming down his cheek and which he rubbed away angrily with the back of his hand.

'Chi's safe!' his mother said. 'That's the main thing, Lee. You have to keep remembering that.'

Lee turned his face to the blank wall. 'How do I *know* that – with her halfway across the world?'

'You know it in your heart, Lee.'

'It's not the same.'

'No,' Mother agreed, 'but it's all we have and we must hold on to that. If we don't, we have nothing. Now, go to sleep.'

Lee fell into another fitful sleep and this time in his dreams, he watched the bowl of incense which Chi had placed in the water for her drowned brother Quan. Slowly, very slowly it bobbed gently over the horizon.

FIVE

Lee woke early, because he was cold, but he piled his anorak on top of the bedclothes and went back to sleep. Around eight Kim banged on his door and poked her head round.

'Come on, sleepy!' she said brightly.

'Go away,' Lee mumbled from beneath a tumble of bedclothes.

'It's time to get up,' Kim insisted.

'I don't want to.'

'Father won't like that.'

Lee hauled his tousled head out and heaved a pillow at Kim. 'Leave me alone! he shouted, but Kim had slammed the door long before the pillow arrived and he tunnelled his way back under the mass of sheets and blankets.

An hour later he stuck his wrist in the air and peered at the figures on his digital watch. 'Nine o'clock?' The block was amazingly silent. 'Where is everybody?' Then he remembered it was Monday, the one day when his father wouldn't bother him because his parents and grandmother had an early morning 'Everyday English' class straight after breakfast.

That was a laugh, Lee thought, teaching his deaf grandmother English as she barely understood Vietnamese, even when it was shouted at her! His mother might benefit from learning the shopping phrases, but of what use could it possibly be to his father? In Cholon he'd been a much respected man, university-educated and acknowledged to have a fine legal mind. Lee's mother had often said, and Lee had no difficulty in believing her, that Father could have gone on to be a barrister if he'd chosen. What good would 'How much are your chickens?' do him? And, even if he had succeeded in learning English, he'd never be able to practise Law again. He knew nothing of English Law. Father had sacrificed his whole life for his children.

'I did it all for you three,' he'd freely admitted when they were still in Hong Kong. 'There is no future for you now in

45

Vietnam, we had to leave to get a better life for you.'

'Is this the better life?' Lee asked himself, as he lay on his back looking at the vague images projected on the ceiling by daylight streaming through the curtains' faded flower pattern.

He listened very hard. There was no sign of life. It was so quiet he could hear the echoing drip of the tap in the bathroom at the end of the corridor.

Though Lee was cold and hungry, he couldn't be bothered to get up and get even colder in the time it would take him to get dressed. Instead he rolled himself tightly into a sausage of bedclothes.

Breakfast would be over anyway. He'd have to buy something from the shop to tide him over until lunch-time.

The day stretched endlessly before him, just like every other day. Lately he'd had more and more difficulty in raising any enthusiasm for getting up. A deep lethargy was settling over him like a shroud, just as it had over most of the others who'd been there as long as the Nguyen family.

'Why do now what you can put off until the next day or the next?' had become the camp motto after two years of living with ever-decreasing hopes of ever getting out.

Movement outside his window produced a blurred, fast-moving dark streak across Lee's ceiling, followed by the banging of the outer door and echoing footsteps approaching down the corridor.

A heavy hand knocked on his door. Phong poked his head round. He was a boy of about Lee's age, though much thinner. Phong was the sole survivor from a family of seven and one of only six to be rescued when their boat capsized at sea. He shared a room at the far end of C Block with another boy who'd made the journey to Hong Kong alone, paid for by his parents. They were desperate for him to leave, though too ill to make the trip themselves.

'The post's in!' Phong shouted. Why Phong, the person least likely to receive a letter, should watch the post so closely was a mystery. He not only knew exactly when it arrived but also who hadn't collected their mail. 'You've got a letter from America and there's another for your father from Hong Kong.' His message delivered, Phong instantly withdrew his head and padded off down the corridor to make his next call.

Lee rolled out of bed and sat shivering on the square of curling carpet while he pulled on the nearest available clothes. He knew the letter must be from Chi. Nobody else wrote to him from America.

Immediately after they separated, when there had still been a slender chance that he might follow her to America, if not to San Francisco, Lee had written regularly. Shortly after the decision came through that the Nguyens would come to England, the correspondence had begun to decline.

At first Lee had convinced himself that Chi's letters were fewer because she had so much to do, to get used to in her new homeland. On those grounds he'd managed for a while to be pleased for her and suppressed his own stirrings of jealousy. But as the gaps between each of her cheery letters grew longer, he almost came to dread their arrival and his replies, with so little news to tell, became more and more difficult to write.

He couldn't help wondering if Chi was outgrowing their long-distance friendship. Maybe his mother had been right when she'd suggested it was better that he should forget her. Chi must soon tire of his everlasting complaints about living in England. Lee had tried to keep those to a minimum, but when he did he seemed to have nothing to say at all and the letters looked abruptly short. Anyway, surrounded by the enchantment of living for three years in the States, her memories of everything they'd shared in the past must be fading quickly.

Dressed in a tracksuit top, the jeans he'd worn the previous day, and with a scarf wound round his neck, Lee found he'd run out of excuses for skulking in his room.

Slowly he emerged into the daylight, crossed the grass and joined the path that ran between the tennis courts and the lecture rooms where his parents were wrestling with the mysteries of English. Having entered the main building through the back door, he made his way to the recreation-hall, where he'd played table tennis the previous night. Off this was a small room which dealt with incoming mail and outgoing parcels.

Hung and one of the English volunteers were on duty. Hung's presence in the post room was one of the main reasons why Lee's father rarely collected mail. During the boat journey Hung, whose main job had been to look after the rationing of their meagre water supplies, had provided one *tael* of gold to buy a new piston for their broken engine. Sadly Father had been duped by the Chinese dealer who'd sold them back their old cracked piston and made off with the money. Lee's father had undertaken personally to repay Hung's gold.

He'd paid off some of that debt while they were in Hong Kong but since they'd arrived in England they'd been living off DHSS cheques and most of that paid for their food and accommodation, leaving them with a meagre amount of pocket money. To his embarrassment, Father still hadn't wiped out the rest of the debt.

Lee didn't have to ask for his letter. The moment he appeared in the hatch Hung handed over the long thin envelope.

'Aren't you going to open it and read it out to us?' Hung asked with a grin.

Lee didn't answer. He glanced briefly at the familiar stamps and Chi's neat, black writing, and stuffed it into his tracksuit pocket, zipping it firmly shut.

So conscious was he of the letter, as he wandered along to the shop, that it almost felt as if it would burn a hole in his chest. Finding some change rattling round in his pockets and determined to delay opening Chi's letter for as long as possible he bought some chocolate and a carton of orange.

This deliberate delay had long been part of a ritual, savouring the moment, hugging the thrill to himself for as long as possible, but that was no longer the case. Nowadays his reason for postponing the act, though he didn't even admit it to himself, was his fear of the contents.

Every time a letter arrived he believed it would be the one that finally extinguished his only remaining dream when Chi explained that she'd met another boy.

He wasn't a fool. It was nearly three years since they'd parted. Several thousand miles separated them; they no longer even shared the same continent and, if he was honest, there was little prospect of them meeting again for the rest of their lives.

Lee took his drink and his chocolate outside, heading towards the wooden post and rail perimeter fence. He climbed the fence and dropped into the grass field beyond. Sometimes there were sheep in the field, but today it was empty.

To his right he could see the backs of a row of houses. Occasionally village children wandered across the field and dared each other to climb the camp fence, but they had only to see a Vietnamese in the distance to scramble back and run for home as fast as their legs could carry them.

One summer, when Lee had been lying in the field, hidden by some deep grass, gazing up at the blue sky and daydreaming himself back to Vietnam, an English boy of about six had come careering across the field so fast that he practically fell over Lee.

For a second the little boy had frozen and then, to Lee's amazement, he'd begun to scream loud enough to wake the district. When Lee had sat up and stretched out a hand to comfort him, the child must have thought Lee intended to harm him. The boy screamed even louder, tears streaming from his tightly closed eyes down his grubby, red jersey.

From nowhere the boy's mother, a big woman with bright blonde hair, had appeared. She snatched the boy away and shouted at Lee, as if he was a mad dog. 'Keep away! Don't you touch him! Keep away.'

Seconds later they'd disappeared back through a gap in the fence into the safety of their own garden, though the woman was still shouting and screaming long after Lee retreated to the camp grounds.

Lee had found the experience very depressing. What was it about him, Lee wondered, that so terrified the child and had made its mother so aggressive in his defence? Surely not the simple difference of the colour of their skins? Did that turn him into some kind of devil? Was his foreignness so frightening?

Because of the uneasy relationship between the refugees and the locals, this field, this no-man's-land, had one distinct advantage, it was the one place where he could go and be certain of being alone. It was here he always brought Chi's letters, determined to be alone in case he found himself reading the dreaded words. He felt every letter brought that day a step closer.

A thorny hedge, thick enough to keep the wind off him, ran down the side of the field furthest from the houses and there Lee squatted on a tussock of grass. He drank the orange and ate the whole bar of chocolate. Now there was nothing else left to do. He'd run out of excuses. His hand shook slightly as he tugged open the zip of his tracksuit pocket and pulled out the envelope. He read his name on the front. Turned the envelope over and read Chi's address on the back, which had not changed.

Then Lee carefully inserted his forefinger into the slit, ripped the envelope open and pulled out the two thin sheets of paper so suddenly that he almost tore them.

The envelope fluttered to the ground as his hand flattened the sheets of paper on his knees. His eye hunted feverishly across the first page for some tell-tale word of excuse, apology, or farewell. Finding none, but still not trusting the contents, which were written in English, Lee turned to the second sheet. Only when he found the tiny kisses arranged in a neat heart around her name at the end did he settle to reading it properly.

Dear Lee,

I hope you are well, I am. I'm sorry it's a while since I last wrote. We've been very busy fixing up the new house. Dad wasn't going to let me help with the painting, but baby Minh kept them awake all night with his teething. Now Dad's working at the Bus Depot and Mum's at my uncle's restaurant every evening they don't have much time. So they let me have a go! Dad reckons I've done 'quite a good job' (high praise from him!) 'for a girl'!!

They're going to let me choose the colours for my room. (Dad said, 'As long as it isn't purple or black!') I've found a real cool yellow I think will do just fine. As you know, my room is at the back of the house, looking out over the yard. Dad wants us to have a patio, a fish pool with a fountain and a barbecue out there, which would be neat, but I think there are a few things we need before we get that!

Any news about your finding a house yet? You mustn't give up hope, Lee. I know things are more difficult in the UK at the moment, but I'm certain everything will work out. You sounded real depressed in your last letter. You really mustn't give up hope after we've all come so far.

Every day when I remember what happened to my brothers I know how lucky I am just to be alive. Now that my parents are getting settled and they've got their new baby boy, they're beginning to treat me more like a human being again too. So you've got to believe that things work themselves out in the end.

Dad has, at long last, reluctantly agreed to me wearing Levis. I bought my first pair last week. After wanting them for so long, when I first put them on I felt really weird! I was too frightened to come out of my bedroom for ages, in case he changed his mind when he saw them, but he didn't say a word. Mum told me later she thought I looked great in them, 'like a real American girl'!

And another thing, because I got an A for my science project, Dad even let me go alone to the High School Prom last week! Is this a major blow for Vietnamese feminism, or what?

You haven't mentioned tennis at all in any of your last three letters. You seemed so keen a while back when you won those trophies and I remember how well you were doing in Hong Kong when Thieu said you could have a real future in it if you really committed yourself to the game. I know it won't be easy to find somebody else to replace Quoc but promise me you will try.

I know we're a long way apart, but we'll always be close in our hearts and minds. I've never forgotten sitting beside you during the voyage to Hong Kong and I'll never forget the time we spent together in Sham Shui Po. Like the evening we went out into Kowloon for our first ever Big Macs! You held my hand all the way there. On the way back, when it started to rain, you slipped your windcheater round my shoulders and then, the best bit of all, you held my face in your hands as you kissed me for the very first time.

Nobody can steal those memories from us.

Don't worry so much! I don't know how, but I know we'll be together again one day, I just know it.

For ever,

Your,

Chi   X   X   X

Lee folded the letter, retrieved the envelope and stuffed it back into his tracksuit pocket. For a while he sat thinking about what Chi had said. The last bit had been good, though he found it impossible to be as optimistic as she was about their future, but he felt guilty about the tennis. How would he ever be able to confess to Chi that he'd wasted their best opportunity of getting to America because he was too busy enjoying the match to think about discussing sponsorship?

Something else, which lay unsaid between the lines of the letter, gnawed at Lee's innards. Who took her to the High School Prom? What did she wear? If she was wearing jeans now, who knew what outrageous, revealing outfits she might wear to a dance?

But beyond simple jealousy, the feeling which overwhelmed Lee was one of being left behind. In every letter Chi wrote she sounded more and more American and less Vietnamese. The slang she'd picked up, the fact that these days she always wrote to him in English, all added up to a growing sense of his falling further and further back in a race in which he'd failed to get off the blocks when the starting pistol went off.

While her parents had got a house, they'd both got jobs and Chi was obviously doing well at school, Lee and his family languished in the camp. While Chi was starting to write and live like an American, doing well in her schooling, though he was having basic English lessons, the rest of his education trailed behind in the wake of that and he wouldn't have the opportunity to attend a college until they had their own home. Chi was becoming a fully-fledged citizen of the United States, whilst four years after he'd left Vietnam Lee's status was still that of a refugee in a foreign country.

He wandered back to the camp, clambered over the fence and went off to join his English class because although he found conversation easier, his grammar needed a good deal of work.

It was lunch-time in the dining-hall before Lee caught up with the rest of his family. Tam was chanting over and over again an English nursery rhyme she'd learned; Kim was mooning over a new student who'd just joined her class and even

Father was looking pleased. 'This morning your mother collected a letter from Uncle Loc!'

Uncle Loc, Father's brother, having helped them to raise the money for their exodus, was the one who had volunteered to stay behind in Vietnam when it was discovered they hadn't got enough to pay for all their passages on the boat. He'd argued that because he had no children, he was unmarried, there was less need for him to go.

'I'll struggle by somehow and one day I'll be able to join you in your new home.'

At the time they'd left he owned a fish shop in Cholon and was saving a reasonable amount of money, but soon after the authorities closed down his shop. Then they began to doubt he would ever save enough to buy a place on a boat out.

Lee's father had sent a constant stream of goods from Hong Kong. All things that Loc would be easily able to sell on the black market to raise funds. Nescafé and toothpaste were particularly highly-prized as they were in very short supply, so were American cigarettes. They'd tried sending packs of cigarettes but the Vietnamese customs officers stole them, so they resorted to slipping several cigarettes inside letters. The coffee, too, was sent in flat plastic bags rather than in the original, but more noticeable, jars.

Twenty months had passed before Uncle Loc escaped and arrived in Hong Kong. By the time he'd gone through quarantine and joined them at Sham Shui Po the family were already preparing for their departure to the UK and Loc's papers couldn't be processed in time for him to travel with them. Once again he'd got left behind.

Knowing that the relatives of the extended family, uncles, cousins and aunts, were permitted to join them under UK immigration rules, Father assumed his brother wouldn't have long to wait, but they hadn't reckoned with the British government's red tape!

Despite repeated applications on Uncle Loc's behalf two years had passed and he was still in Hong Kong, though no longer in Sham Shui Po. Recently he'd been moved to a closed camp on Lantau Island.

First, the Home Office lost Father's application form and, when that was sorted out, nobody could find Loc's papers in Hong Kong. Eventually it turned out there were three other people in Lantau with similar names and they'd been processing the wrong papers!

'Is Uncle Loc coming to join us?' Lee asked.

'Not yet,' Father admitted, 'but he's been told that his papers are coming through and he must be ready to leave.'

'I think he's better off where he is,' Lee said, as he ate his rice and fish. He never tasted fish without remembering how much he'd eaten during their voyage when fish was the only fresh protein available. Months after they'd arrived in Hong Kong Lee slowly grew used to the flavour again, though it never tasted as fresh as the ones he'd caught with his grandfather.

'Better off where he is?' said Father. 'Of course not! Why do you say that?'

'At least he's amongst his own kind.'

Father gestured around the dining-hall. 'So are we.'

'Not for very much longer. One day we'll be allocated a house and we'll have to go and live in the outside world.'

'There are Chinese and Vietnamese out there too,' Father pointed out.

'The Chinese in the UK don't want to know us! Most of them had to save up for years to come over from Hong Kong and when they arrived they had to make their own way. They think with our flights paid for and the special camps set up for us to live in, not to mention the extra education we get, that we've had it too easy!'

'Yes, but there are the Vietnamese already outside.'

'But look what happened to Quoc's family. They were given a council house in Cleveland because there was so much unemployment that no English people wanted to live there. The nearest Vietnamese family lives nearly a hundred miles away. What chance have they got of ever meeting up? Besides which, they've got almost nothing in common. Quoc's father was a surgeon in Saigon, the other family were fishermen in North Vietnam.'

Father nodded. 'I know all of that. Things can be very

54

difficult, isolated, but you have to consider the alternative.'

Lee shrugged. 'All I said was, Uncle Loc is probably better off in Hong Kong.'

'Times have changed,' Father said, 'even in Hong Kong. You can no longer work outside the camps, the way Kim and you did. Unemployment has grown there too and the local community feel it is unfair that we Vietnamese, who have homes and food provided for us, should be taking the jobs they need. The world has forgotten Vietnam and countries are no longer willing to accept more and more refugees. The Hong Kong authorities have so many Vietnamese in the camps that they've tried voluntary repatriation but too few people accepted. Soon they'll be forcibly sending people back to Vietnam, whether they want to go or not!'

Lee finished his food. 'Maybe we should never have left. Things weren't so bad there.'

'You forget,' Father said sadly.

But his mother hadn't. 'What about the time they took your father away six months out into the country, to one of their New Economic Zones and made him work with his bare hands, preparing the land for crops?'

'Mother, Lee was too young to really know what was happening!'

'I remember you being away.'

Mother nodded. 'But do you remember me taking things from the house to sell, so that we could buy rice on the black market because we were starving?'

'Well, I know we're not starving here, but how much better off are we?'

'I keep telling you,' Father said patiently, 'we have freedom, freedom to think and do what we like.'

Lee rose to leave. 'But it seems to me we're still a minority, just as we were in Vietnam and in Hong Kong. The Vietnamese didn't like us for our Chinese origins and in Hong Kong the Chinese didn't like us because we were Vietnamese! Here we're still a minority at the bottom of the pile and no minority ever got the best of a deal. Not unless they were Royalty!'

Lee began to walk off down the hall. Kim called after him. 'I know why you're in such a bad mood. You had a letter from Chi today, didn't you?'

'That's none of your business. Just leave me alone.'

As he swept out into the cold, fresh air a jumble of desperate thoughts tumbled through his mind; of returning to Vietnam with the Morning Star Battalion or better still, of stowing away on a boat bound for America so that he could rejoin Chi and pick up the threads of a totally new life. Either way he knew that somehow he had to get out of the camp but how could he get anywhere without any money? He'd never get to an English port in the first place, let alone to America!

Then as he stuffed his hands deep into his jeans' pockets, he found the two ten-pound notes he'd won from Bill Keever. He'd intended to hand the money over to his father, but when the row about a sponsor had broken out he'd forgotten all about it.

So, he *had* money after all!

SIX

The following day he'd joined Kim and several other refugees in the camp minibus and gone into the nearest town. Anything to get out of the camp for a few hours. Whilst Kim and the other passengers shopped in the supermarket, Lee walked down the High Street, ignoring the curious and occasionally hostile glances he received.

On the end of a row of shops was one which he thought of as typically English, perhaps because of its Victorian bow-window. Through the tiny panes of glass he could see dark, antique furniture. Old fly-blown pictures and gilt mirrors hung on the walls.

But the sole object of Lee's interest lay on a glass shelf, just inside the window, where a selection of jewellery and trinkets was displayed. Amongst the earrings, cuff links and costume jewellery was a plain, gold wedding ring.

When the pirates had robbed their boat, amongst the many things they'd stolen had been his grandmother's wedding ring. She'd sworn it wasn't even real gold and resisted the pirate until the last second. The pirate brandishing his knife had said, if she didn't hand it over he'd take her finger with it.

She'd quietly pulled off the ring and tossed it on to the deck rather than hand it directly to the man and forced him to demean himself by having to bend down to pick it up.

Lee had so much admired his grandmother's spirit that he'd vowed to himself that one day he would replace the ring. That was what Grandfather would have done if he'd lived and Lee felt bound to take on that responsibility.

He'd seen that particular ring in the shop window on previous visits, but this time he plucked up the courage to enter the shop.

The old-fashioned shop bell was still jangling when a little woman, not much younger than his grandmother, with bright blue eyes and a pink, hooked nose bustled out from the back of the shop through a heavily-curtained doorway. She stopped dead in her tracks the second she saw Lee, but recovered enough to snap, 'Yes?'

'Is this gold?' Lee was standing just inside the door by the window and as he spoke he was about to reach over and point at the ring.

'Don't touch!' the woman snapped.

Lee jumped back as if he'd been given an electric shock. 'Sorry?'

'Don't like people touching me belongings,' she grumbled, forcing herself between Lee and the tray of jewellery, giving him a faint whiff of lavender. 'You can handle the goods to your heart's content once you've bought them! Is what gold?'

'That ring.'

The woman snatched it up off the tray. 'This, is this gold? I should say so,' she said without bothering to look at it more closely. 'Ten pounds, take it or leave it.'

Lee was about to take the ring, to examine it more closely, but her hand snapped shut as sharply as a mousetrap, clearly believing he intended to snatch it from her and run off without paying. Her fist was clenched so tightly that her knuckles went white.

Lee wrestled with his conscience. He desperately wanted to buy Grandmother the ring, but if he did, it would take half the money he had, money which could be his ticket out of the camp. Had this all happened two weeks earlier he wouldn't have hesitated to buy the ring but now he had a different set of priorities. Not having handled much English money he had only a hazy idea what twenty pounds would buy, he just knew it was more than he'd ever had since he arrived in England, or was likely to see again for some time.

'Hurry up! I haven't got all day,' the old woman snapped.

Lee couldn't see her urgency, there was nobody else in the shop, in fact though many people looked in the window he'd never seen anybody in there.

'Do you want it or not?' she demanded.

Flustered, Lee couldn't make up his mind. If this had been a shop in Cholon, or Hong Kong, he would have had the confidence to haggle to bring her price down, but English shopkeepers didn't seem to understand the custom.

'I have not enough money,' he lied.

'Then be off with you,' she said, opening the door for him and almost pushing him through it. 'The very idea, coming in wasting my time!'

The shop door slammed behind him and Lee made his way back down the street to the waiting minibus.

'What did you buy?' Kim asked.

'Nothing,' Lee said with a shrug.

'I got nail varnish remover, shampoo and a new deodorant.'

'Thank goodness, you were beginning to smell awful!' Lee said with a grin and then ducked to avoid her blow.

When they got back to the camp Lee was strolling back to C Block when Nancy Keever called him over. 'Lee, you went into town on the minibus this morning, didn't you?'

'Yes, why?'

Nancy looked puzzled. 'It's just that we've had a rather weird phone call from the police.'

Lee froze. Any mention of police, to him, meant trouble. Of course it wasn't the same as being in Vietnam, where the police seemed to make up the law as they went along, but any intervention by the authorities might delay their departure from the transit camp even longer.

Nancy continued, 'Some woman in an antique shop rang them and said that one of our people had been in threatening her and trying to steal a gold ring.'

Lee kept looking straight at Nancy, trying to give nothing away. Why had the woman lied? Maybe he *had* frightened her, but that hadn't been his intention.

'You didn't happen to see anyone around that shop, did you Lee?'

'I don't know the shop,' he lied. He knew he'd done nothing wrong, the woman was lying, but he didn't want to become involved in lengthy explanations that might be misunderstood.

'Oh, it's got an Olde Worlde type window and it's up the far end of the High Street.'

'I didn't go down that end of the town.'

'Oh, it's probably nothing really. After all nothing was actually stolen, but when the police ring we have to check it out.

59

The Camp Director took the call just before he left for a meeting and because I run the minibus service, he's asked me for a list of this morning's passengers. I'll ask around some of the others.'

As Nancy turned to go, Lee wished he hadn't lied. What if somebody had seen him heading in that direction?

'By the way, Lee ...'

Lee stopped in his tracks and turned to face Nancy.

' ... Pop said to say how much he enjoyed your game of tennis yesterday.'

'Oh, thank you, it was fun.'

'No, really, it was much more than that for him. Pop really knows his stuff when it comes to tennis. He was very impressed with your game and said you're extremely talented and you've got terrific potential.'

Lee felt himself blushing.

'As a matter of fact you and your family seemed to be his main topic of conversation at dinner last night. He talked of little else!'

'When will your father be coming here again?' Lee asked. 'I'd like another match with him and to introduce him to my father.'

Nancy shook her head. 'I doubt he'll be here again for quite a while. This was his first visit to the UK for a couple of years, he's a very busy man.'

Gloomily Lee began to walk away but an idea struck him. 'He said he was going back on Friday?'

'That's right.'

'Where's he staying in London, please?'

'He's the guest of the American ambassador and he's spending a great deal of time at the United States embassy in Grosvenor Square. Why?'

Lee tried to pass it off as unimportant. 'I thought I'd write and thank him for the game.'

'Oh, sure, but today's Tuesday and the post's gone so you might easily miss him,' Nancy pointed out. 'You'd do better to send the letter to the States. I'll write the address out and give it to you.'

Though he was disappointed that Bill wouldn't get his letter immediately, Lee decided he must still write it straight away while the idea was fresh in his mind. He was back in his room, trying to frame the contents in his head, when he heard a scream of anguish coming from one of the bathrooms.

Kim, anxious to try out her new shampoo, had commandeered it the moment she got back.

Lee joined several other people in the corridor as they made their way towards the bathroom and banged on the door.

'What's the matter?' they cried.

Kim's voice, rather shaky, answered. 'Nothing, it's all right, go away!'

'Are you sure?' Lee called out.

'Yes, go away!'

They all wandered back to their rooms but Lee, listening out for any further trouble, followed Kim to her room the second he heard the door close. He remembered to knock and when he opened the door he found Kim drying her hair with a towel.

'Go away,' she shouted, 'leave me alone!'

'But what was all the fuss about?' he asked.

'Nothing, mind your own business.'

'"Nothing" can't make you scream that loud!' Lee said scornfully. 'Not another spider, was it?'

Kim looked sulky. 'I just gave myself a shock, if you must know.'

'How?

'I sprayed underneath my arms with my new deodorant,' she held up the aerosol can.

'So what?'

'It isn't deodorant, that's what!'

Lee grinned. 'What is it?'

'Hair spray!'

Lee fell on the bed laughing.

'Don't you dare tell anyone,' she said angrily.

'But how on earth could you do such a thing?' he asked eventually.

'One of the other girls showed me which one she used, only the printing on hers was in yellow and this one's red, but it's got the same name on the front!'

Lee took the can from her and examined it. 'But that's the

name of the company that makes them both,' he explained and pointed with a finger to the smaller print beneath. 'This says what's in the can. Hair spray! Fancy having stiff armpits!'

'It's not funny!' Kim insisted. 'It stung me and it isn't that easy to get off either!'

'I'm sorry, I didn't mean to laugh,' he said. 'Poor Kim! It's a strange country we're living in,' he added as he left.

Walking back to his room Lee wondered how they thought they'd ever survive in the outside world if they couldn't even tell the contents of one aerosol from another? What if it had been something really serious, like a danger warning that they didn't understand?

He sat down at his rickety table with a sheet of the notepaper to write to Bill. Apart from practising for job applications as part of his English class, the only other letters he'd written in English were to Chi, which didn't help him to get started on this one. 'Dear Mr Keever', as his teacher had instructed, looked too formal but 'Dear Bill' didn't sound right either.

Lee sighed. Better to concentrate on the rest of the letter, he could go back and deal with the opening later. But the rest didn't prove any easier. He'd told Nancy it was just a thank-you letter, and that was his excuse for writing, but what he really wanted to do, tactfully, was to raise the subject of sponsorship. But he couldn't think how to do that without making it sound like a begging letter.

As he gazed round, seeking inspiration from his bleak room he noticed Chi's letter lying on the floor by his bed. He'd read it over and over again in a desperate attempt to squeeze from it the last drop of information. But each time he read it, the more his mind began to twist the words until the meaning became frighteningly distorted.

Far from being a comfort, he found the letter disturbed him more and more each time he read it. There was something she'd said about the High School Prom which particularly bothered him. He was positive this wasn't the first time she'd mentioned the dance and her father refusing to allow her to go. But there was something else ...

Lee knelt in front of the wardrobe and searched about in the bottom for a cardboard box which had once contained a pair of trainers and now housed his complete collection of letters from Chi. Everything she'd ever written to him, every postcard and photograph she'd sent had been carefully filed in the box, which was almost full.

His fingers ran along the tops of the envelopes until he found one she'd posted around the same date in the previous year.

Also read and re-read, this letter, too, was worn-looking and slightly grubby from the number of times he'd handled it. He unfolded the pages. She'd written much more in those days, and his eye ran through the paragraphs until he found what he was looking for.

'Warren wanted to take me to the High School Prom.'

Warren! There was no mention of Warren in her latest letter, but maybe she'd deliberately left out that *minor* detail?

Lee remembered Chi had mentioned Warren somewhere else, something to do with her learning English.

Yes, here it was!

'Dad got mad because I've been stopping off at the coffee bar on my way home from school, but I explained Warren was helping me with my English and then Dad didn't mind so much.'

And in another letter there was another reference, when Chi was talking about starting to work on her science project. The project she'd got an A for this term, the very A which had persuaded her father to let her go to the Prom at all!

'I got in a terrible muddle, but Warren was very kind and helped me to sort it all out.'

Warren seemed to be doing a great deal for Chi!

Maybe Warren was in one of the photographs she'd sent. Several were informal class photographs, including other students, and Lee was positive that at least one had been taken in somewhere like a coffee bar. When he'd first seen the photographs he'd hardly had eyes for anyone but Chi. Now he went through them more carefully.

He found the photograph he was looking for.

There was Chi, looking very happy for somebody who was supposed to miss him so much! Four other people were in the photograph, sitting at a red table with tall glass dishes of ice cream in front of them. None of the others was Vietnamese. Two of them were girls, though not as attractive as Chi, but there were also two boys. One had light brown hair, the other blond. The blond boy wore his hair long and floppy and he had glasses, big ones that made him look like an owl.

All the people in the photograph were smiling, but there was something else Lee hadn't noticed before, the blond boy was the only one not looking towards the camera. His head was turned away so that he was looking straight at Chi with a very sloppy look on his face.

Was that Warren? And had he succeeded, where he failed last year, in taking Chi to the High School Prom?

Irritably Lee stuffed all the letters back into the box, not bothering about the order any more. He was putting the box back in the wardrobe when he heard Grandmother's raised voice coming through the wall as she laid down the law to her son. 'This isn't how I expected to spend my old age!'

Father agreed. 'It won't be for much longer.'

'What?'

Father raised his voice and in doing so the words lost their air of comfort. 'I said, it won't be for long.'

'Two years we've been living in this hell hole.'

'I know.'

'What?'

'I KNOW!'

'You promised me a new life,' she grumbled, 'this is worse than the old one.'

Lee slipped a cassette of traditional Vietnamese music into his radio and turned it on to drown out the argument. He decided to tidy out his wardrobe, after all he wasn't getting very far with the letter to Bill.

Setting aside the box of Chi's letters he began to dig deeper into the mess. Almost the first object he came across was the shiny black-handled clasp knife. The main blade was rusting, it was some time since he'd needed to use it. As he pulled out the various gadgets, the corkscrew, the fish disgorger and several others he'd never discovered the real purpose of, Lee's mind drifted back to the reason his grandfather had given it to him.

Lee had gone to his grandparents for a summer holiday, not realising they would never be returning to Cholon and Grandfather had presented him with the knife to make up for not hiring a boat to take them on a trip up the coast as they always had in the past. Little did he realise at the time that he would be setting out on the most dangerous and exciting trip of his life within the next few days.

Lee had been on the boat, gliding through the darkness towards the mouth of the estuary, before he'd realised he'd forgotten the knife. It was Grandfather who'd remembered it and had returned it to him on the boat.

Lee turned the knife over in the palm of his hand and set it on one side thinking how different everything had been in those days.

Apart from a half-empty box of matches and a good deal of rubbish, he found little else of interest until he came to the very back of the wardrobe. Right in the furthest corner was a hand line his grandfather had made for him so that Lee could fish over the side of the boat. Every metre it had hooks tied on it and there were lures made from feathers or cut from the silver paper from chewing-gum packs.

It was only as Lee put the line down next to the knife and the matchbox, that he realised he was getting ready for another journey.

The idea flashed into his mind – why write to Bill? He knew he'd never be able to get across what he really wanted to say in a letter. Besides, it was far too important for that. It was time to take positive action! Tomorrow was Wednesday, somehow he'd get to London and talk to Bill Keever personally.

Fired by this thought, Lee raced over to J Block in search of Tran though when he found him he tried to appear very casual. 'When you go to London,' Lee asked, 'how do you get there?'

Tran laughed. 'As you can see, I don't have wings. Sometimes I go by train or bus but if I haven't got much money I hitchhike. You know,' he stuck his thumb up, 'get lifts. Lorry drivers are the best. With cars you never know where they're going, so you can't tell if it's worth stopping them or not. The best place to try is by the motorway. Hey, what's all this about? What would you want in London?'

Confused, Lee hastily found an excuse. 'Not London, I don't want to go there, but I was thinking of going to visit Quoc,' he lied.

'Do you know his address?'

'I'll get it from Nancy. All I know is, it's in a place called Cleveland.'

'That's in the opposite direction to London,' Tran said scathingly, 'near the border with Scotland.'

'I know that!'

But as he walked back to his room Lee wasn't thinking about his knowledge of the geography of Britain, which he had to admit was rather sketchy, he was deciding to keep the whole idea of his visit to London a secret from his family. He knew they would only try to talk him out of it.

But he did write to Chi. He explained his idea about how he was going to see Bill Keever to talk about him sponsoring them and he also asked some detailed questions about who she had gone to the Prom with and whether she had seen much of Warren lately?

There was something very final about sealing the letter. Having told Chi about the journey he was now committed to going.

SEVEN

An hour and a half after he'd walked through the camp gate Lee reached the outskirts of the town he'd visited the previous day. Although it had taken him ages compared to the brief journey in the minibus he was still beginning to feel quite cheerful. Not only had the sun broken through the cloud but the further from the camp he got the freer he felt, freer than he'd been for years. For a few days at least he wouldn't be subject to camp rules and regulations or have to listen to the constant discussions about when they'd be allocated a house and the bickering which sprang from them.

There was even a taste of danger about stepping off alone into the unknown, a flavour he hadn't experienced since their arrival in Hong Kong. Even the fear that at any moment, because he was still so close to the camp, he might be spotted and taken back, gave added spice to his adventure.

Leaving his family without a word did have its down side but the main point was, he was finally *doing* something instead of sitting around in the camp waiting for others, in their own good time, to decide his future.

All he had to do now was keep well away from the antique shop and its vindictive owner, he certainly didn't want her spotting him and ringing the police again, and find the road out which led to the motorway.

It was some time since he'd last gone that way, on an outing to a swimming pool, and he couldn't quite remember the right direction. There were five roads leaving town, including the one he'd arrived on, and he'd walked some way up two of them, turned back and tried again, before he passed a garage he recognised and knew he'd found the right one.

Lee was quite relieved when he'd passed the last of the houses. People kept staring at him. Old men in gardens pushing lawnmowers stopped their work, eased their backs and watched him go by. Women hanging out washing didn't turn their heads, but he was convinced their eyes swivelled in his direction the moment his back was turned. There was a constant feeling of being watched. Even from houses where he saw nobody.

Once out of the town the pavement quickly ended. The road was no narrower than the one he'd used in from the camp but with no verge at all he was forced to walk in the uneven gutter and the traffic, particularly the speeding lorries with their vicious after-draught, was much heavier.

Two lorries, one from each direction, were due to meet right by him. The one on his side of the road couldn't pull out to avoid him without crashing into the other. Terrified, Lee pressed himself into the hedgebank. Hawthorn scratching his face and tearing at his anorak, he was convinced that the lorry was bound to hit him, but it applied its brakes and with a great snorting of compressed air, stopped just in time.

After the other lorry had gone safely by and the one that had stopped swung out to pass him, a boy not much older than Lee, wound down the window and stuck his red face out.

'Why don't you go back where you come from?' the lad shouted angrily and the lorry drove off leaving Lee coughing miserably in a cloud of blue diesel fumes.

'I'm trying!' Lee said out loud. 'I'm trying!'

Lee decided the road was too dangerous to walk along and climbed over a gate and tried to make his way across the fields inside the hedge. It wasn't as easy as he'd expected. The fields were not only uneven, some had crops of standing corn ripening in them, though others were grassland, but they were also quite small and each was separated from the next either by another hedge, or by a fence, both of which usually had vicious strands of barbed wire to negotiate that tore at his clothes and hands. Some of the hedges he met proved impenetrable and he was forced to make long detours through gates which doubled the distance and slowed his progress down.

At twelve o'clock he gave up, sat under a tree and took his first break of the day. He ate some of the cold chicken, drank some juice and finished his lunch off with part of a chocolate bar. He was sorry he'd chosen to bring juice in cartons because he had no alternative but to finish it and he only had one other carton left.

He wished now he hadn't been so anxious to get out of the town and had stayed long enough to buy something to drink in a screw-top bottle which would have meant less waste.

Perhaps he should also have bought more food. Twelve-thirty and he had no idea how far he was from the motorway. The walk was taking much longer than he'd expected. Would he even reach the motorway, let alone get a lift and make London by nightfall? There was nothing for it, but to press on and get as far as he could.

Footsore and very weary, Lee at last reached the slip road that ran up to the motorway by four o'clock. The blue and white sign at the entrance mentioned Birmingham and Stoke but not London. He made his choice. All he had to do now was hitch a lift.

Three-quarters of an hour later Lee was still standing on the dusty hard shoulder beside the slip road. Each time a vehicle passed he extended his arm, thumb pointing up, as Tran had demonstrated. There'd been no shortage of traffic. A constant stream of cars, lorries and even motorbikes poured by. That was the problem. None had shown the least inclination to slow down, let alone offer him a lift.

What bothered Lee most was the occasional red and white police car which would shoot round the roundabout below and surge up the slip road towards him. Not that any of them stopped, but the policeman beside the driver always looked at Lee as if he was making a mental note of a suspicious person.

Having missed lunch, his parents were sure to have looked round the camp to find him. What would they do next? He had gone off on his own before without telling them. So far they might only have casually mentioned his absence to one of the English volunteers, but when he didn't turn up for his evening meal, in just under an hour, they'd almost certainly go to the Camp Director.

An awful thought suddenly crossed Lee's mind. If his father went to the Camp Director, to report Lee missing, would the Director remember the woman's complaint about a Vietnamese who had been trying to steal one of her rings? By now Nancy would have handed in the list of people who'd gone into town yesterday and Lee's name was on that list! Not only that, but he'd lied to Nancy about not being up that end of town and somebody might easily have seen him walking in that direction.

Suppose, when he heard that Lee was missing, the Camp Director put two and two together and believed that it was guilt from the attempted theft of the ring that had forced Lee to run away? Then the police really would be after him!

'Do you want a lift or not?'

Lee had been so deeply involved in his thoughts that he hadn't noticed an old lorry that had passed him and then pulled up.

The driver, his head out of the cab window, shouted back to Lee. 'Come on then, if you're coming!'

Lee ran up the road, scrambled up on to the wheel hub, hauled himself up through the door the driver held open for him and fell into the passenger seat.

The driver, in his thirties, had ginger hair and wore only a grubby white vest above his jeans.

'No luggage, travelling light, eh?'

Lee nodded. Almost before he'd sat down the driver had pushed the gear lever forwards, swung the wheel across and the lorry jerked its way off the hard shoulder back on to the slip road. Moments later they were chugging along in the slow lane behind a furniture lorry.

'Are you going far?' the driver shouted over the noise of the engine and the vibration it set up.

Lee nodded. 'All the way,' he shouted back.

'Eh?' the driver said cupping a hand behind his red ear.

The noise of the old lorry engine was drowning out his words and Lee realised with a smile this was going to be just like trying to have a conversation with his grandmother. 'ALL THE WAY!' he shouted again.

The lorry driver nodded. 'Have you come far?'

'Not far,' Lee said, shaking his head. He didn't want to risk giving anything away.

After that, much to Lee's relief, the driver abandoned all attempt at conversation. He offered Lee a cigarette and, when Lee refused, lit his own and smoked it in silence. He planted one beefy arm on the wound down cab window with the faster traffic zipping past just beyond his pink elbow.

The warmth of the cab, coupled with the constant noise and the familiar, comforting smell of hot engine oil soon made Lee drowsy. His eyelids drooped. Ten minutes up the motorway he was fast asleep, his head back on the greasy, black lorry seat.

In the middle of a frightening dream about being chased down the High Street by the angry woman from the antique shop and just at the moment when a policeman's hand came down heavily on his shoulder, Lee woke to find the lorry driver shaking him.

'Want a cuppa?'

Lee rubbed his eyes and looked round. The lorry was parked amongst many other larger ones on the forecourt of a motorway service station.

'Do you want a cuppa?' the driver repeated.

Still half asleep and never having heard the word before Lee was baffled.

'Please?'

The man raised his eyes to heaven and then mimed drinking. 'Drink, do you want a drink?' he said slowly and carefully.

'Oh, no thanks. I've got a drink.'

'Well, you'll still have to come with me, whether you want one or not. I can't leave you in the cab and the lorry unlocked, or my boss'll go hairless.'

Although he only understood about one word in every six, Lee got the general idea and hauled himself out. The moment he was out of the warmth of the cab, as he followed the driver across the lorry park towards the café only used by the professional drivers, Lee shivered. The sun was still shining, but what heat there had been seemed to have gone out of it. Glancing at his watch Lee was surprised to discover he'd been asleep for over two hours, it was gone seven o'clock.

Lee had always found the English to be such quiet, formal people who took their pleasures solemnly. They always seemed to eat in silence, only speaking when they had to and then usually in lowered voices, as if they were exchanging secrets in a library! Vietnamese meals were much jollier affairs with everyone laughing and talking, clearly enjoying themselves.

But the moment the driver opened the door Lee realised it was obviously a place where old friends met regularly. Far from sitting stiffly at their own tables, eyes averted, many had turned their chairs sideways and the conversation, punctuated by bursts of loud laughter, seemed to spread right across the room.

Lee, who was also used, at best, to people pretending not to have noticed him, was barely through the door when a gruff voice asked his driver loudly, 'What you picked up there, Scotty – a Chinese takeaway?'

'Hey, leave the kid alone,' Scotty replied firmly, but with a good-humoured grin, as he led the way to the counter. 'Hi, Dawn.'

'Hello, Scotty.' Dawn, a cheerful girl who wore her pink catering cap perched precariously on her piled-up chestnut hair, gave them a broad smile. 'What can I do for you?'

'You could make me a happy man,' Scotty said with a grin, 'but I suppose we'd better just eat!' He turned to Lee. 'What are you having, mate?'

'Nothing, thank you,' Lee said politely, he didn't want to spend his money on food, though in truth he was starving and the smell of food, even English food, was very tempting.

'You can't sit there having nothing,' Scotty said firmly, 'you'll put me off my dinner. Have some chips, you do eat chips, don't you?'

Lee nodded.

'And a hamburger?'

Lee, remembering that first Big Mac and French Fries he'd bought Chi in Kowloon, agreed.

'And a cup of tea?'

'Please, but no milk.'

Scotty gave him an odd look, but nodded to Dawn. When they got to the checkout Lee pulled out one of his precious ten-pound notes, but Scotty insisted on paying.

They found a couple of places at a table with two older men and, even before Scotty had finished drowning his plate of pie and chips in tomato ketchup, Lee had bitten deeply into his burger.

'So, where were you born?' Scotty asked.

'Vietnam.'

The fat man with dark hair who sat opposite Lee said, 'I had an Australian mate who was in the army out there. Only twenty-two when he got killed by a Vietnamese. Can't say I like them that much.'

'I am not Viet Cong,' Lee said indignantly. 'I am from the south, I was born in Cholon near Saigon. My father worked with the United States army,' Lee said firmly.

The big man didn't seem convinced. 'So what are you doing over here then?'

'When the Americans left Saigon was very bad. No food, no jobs, so we fled.'

'We haven't got any jobs to spare.'

'You don't understand,' Lee said. 'There *were* jobs in Saigon, but they wouldn't let us Chinese who'd worked with the Americans have them.'

'I thought you said you were Vietnamese?'

'Yes,' Lee agreed, 'but my ancestors were Chinese.'

'So you keep wandering from country to country?' The fat man remained unimpressed, obviously seeing them as scavengers.

'My family have lived in Vietnam for hundreds of years,' Lee said proudly.

'Probably longer than your lot have been in England, Bob,' Scotty said to the fat man.

'What do you mean?' Bob demanded indignantly.

'Gallaccio isn't an English name, is it? Where are you from?'

'My grandparents were Italian,' Bob admitted.

'Exactly!' said Scotty.

The fat man laughed uneasily.

The other man, tall with thinning blond hair, who'd been silently listening to the conversation joined in. 'I traced my ancestors once.'

'Oh, yes, and what did you find out?' Scotty asked.

'We Rasmussens came over with the Vikings, killed some people around Scarborough and took all their land.'

'Seems to me,' Scotty said quietly, 'my friend here's got about as much right to be in England as anyone, he just happens to be a bit more noticeable than the rest of us.'

The fat man got up to go. 'I still reckon it ought to be first come first served!' he said and left.

'Don't take any notice,' Scotty said, 'he's all right really.'

'I don't mind,' Lee said, 'I only wish my English was better so that I could explain things better.'

'Finish your tea, we'd best be off, we've a long way to go yet.'

While they'd been eating a steady downpour of rain had set in and they got soaked running back to the lorry. What was worse, when Scotty switched on the engine it refused to start.

'Damn this old crate!' he said fiercely as he turned and turned the engine without its showing the slightest inclination to fire. 'I keep telling my boss this old lorry ought to be on the scrap heap but he's too mean to shell out for a new one.'

'Can you fix it?' Lee asked anxiously. It was past eight and his hopes of being in London by nightfall were fading fast.

'Me, fix it?' Scotty laughed. 'I doubt it. I'm a foundryman by trade not a mechanic! I only took this job when the steel mill packed up.' He opened the cab door. 'You wait here while I go and see if I can find someone to look at it.'

'I know about engines, I'll look at it for you,' Lee offered eagerly.

Scotty looked very doubtful.

'You have been very kind to me,' Lee urged, 'this is one way I can repay you.'

'Thanks all the same, kid, but I think this is a job for the professionals.'

'I worked in garages in Saigon and Hong Kong before I came to England.'

'You did?' Scotty sounded unconvinced. 'No, better not. My boss would sack me if anything happened to this heap of scrap metal of his.'

'Let me look!' Lee pleaded. 'That can't do any harm.'

'I don't know. Oh, go on then! Look, but don't break anything!'

'She's already broken,' Lee said with a grin, 'I can only make her better.'

'I hope you're right!' Scotty said under his breath.

Scotty stood looking anxiously over Lee's shoulder, ignoring the rain that fell on his bare shoulders, while he peered into the engine.

'You turn her over, please?'

Scotty wasn't very happy, leaving Lee alone by the engine, but he realised there was no choice. He turned the engine over twice but when it didn't immediately start he jumped down again.

'Look, kid, I'll go and get somebody ... '

'Have you got a dry cloth?'

'Yes, sure,' Scotty said, impatiently reaching into a compartment in the cab.

With the rag, Lee dried the condensation off the high tension cable, between the coil and the distributor, and then worked his way along each cable from the distributor cap to the spark plugs. He systematically removed and replaced each one, having first dried not only their insulators, but the ceramic part too.

'Okay, try again.'

Still the engine refused to start and Scotty, without wishing to hurt the boy's feelings, wanted to go and get real help. 'It's good of you to try, kid, but ... '

'I think I've found it,' Lee interrupted. 'The shaking of the engine has made the low tension cable from the coil come off.' Lee pushed the spade terminal back on but it was too loose. 'Do you have pliers?'

Scotty delved into the box and handed him a pair. Lee eased back the rubber covering and gently squeezed the metal terminals until the connection was a snug fit.

'Try it now.'

Scotty did and slowly the engine, because the battery had been weakened by their previous attempts, whirred into life and fired. 'Hey, kid,' Scotty shouted over the revving of the engine, 'you're terrific!'

Lee proudly slammed the bonnet down and climbed into the cab wiping the oil off his hands on the rag. 'It was nothing,' he said.

'Soon have you in Glasgow now,' Scotty said, as he slipped the lorry into gear.

75

Lee wasn't sure he'd heard right. 'Glasgow?'

'Sure. That is where you're going, isn't it?'

Lee miserably shook his head. 'No, London.'

'Oh! Well, I've got bad news for you. We're just outside Kendal and you've travelled about a hundred miles in the wrong direction!'

EIGHT

'I thought, when I asked you where you were going, you'd already seen Glasgow painted on the side of my lorry,' Scotty said. 'Didn't you even see the signs on the motorway that said you were standing on the side for the North?'

Lee felt bitterly disappointed at having wasted a whole day on what was now becoming a tight schedule. After all Bill Keever would leave the country the day after tomorrow. 'I was so relieved to have got to the motorway and found a lift, I didn't really look.' He didn't want to admit how vague his knowledge of English geography was.

Scotty rubbed his head. 'What are you going to do now?'

'I will have to go back.'

'But there's no service station on the other side here,' Scotty pointed out, 'and you can't walk across the motorway.'

'Is there a railway station near?'

'We could easily find one,' Scotty said. He felt very sorry for the boy, especially after he'd been good enough to fix the engine. 'Have you got some money?'

'Twenty pounds.'

Scotty shook his head. 'That won't get you to London from here. I'd give you the rest ... '

'No, I couldn't let you,' Lee protested.

'I'd be happy to, for fixing the lorry, but I don't get paid for last week until I get back to the factory and I've hardly a pound left in my pocket. If I'd got a mechanic to the lorry I'd have had to use a credit card. I tell you what, I'll take you on to the next slip road where there's a bridge for you to cross and you'll maybe pick up a lift in the opposite direction.'

There was nothing else for it. Silently they drove to the next turn off and Scotty stopped the lorry on the bridge.

'This is it then, kid,' Scotty shouted over the noise of the engine.

'Thank you,' Lee said as he jumped down on to the road.

'The engine should be all right now, but keep it running just in case until you get back. It will help recharge the battery.'

Scotty laughed, touched by Lee's concern for him when he felt the boot was really on the other foot. 'I'll be all right, kid. Take care, good luck!'

Lee watched the lorry drive off down the slope and rejoin the motorway. As it did Scotty's bare, freckled arm appeared through the open window in a brief wave of farewell. Lee waved back feeling very small and lost. Just when he thought everything had been going so well, too!

Looking around him, as he crossed the bridge with the traffic whizzing beneath him, Lee realised Scotty had dropped him in a fairly desolate spot.

He learned just how desolate during the two hours he stood beside the southbound slip road as few vehicles passed him and none stopped. As the interval between cars grew even longer Lee began to face up to the idea of being stranded.

With a stiff westerly breeze he felt bitterly cold and because of the heavy cloud the light was fading fast. He glanced at his surroundings. Apart from the motorway and the road he was on, Lee could see little but moorland and hills in every direction. There was a large farmhouse almost on the horizon but apart from that the only other man-made object in this bleak landscape was about a hundred metres away, a small, run-down building that had once been whitewashed. It had a single window, a door from which the green paint was peeling and it was surrounded by sheep. At least it might offer some shelter and it was far enough away from the farm for nobody to find him there.

Just after ten Lee thought, 'If I leave it much longer, I won't be able to find the place!' He climbed the fence and dropped down into the field of sheep.

Some of the sheep, believing they were being attacked, scattered, bleating loudly, but some braver and more curious animals, thinking he might have brought food, moved cautiously towards him.

Lee, a city boy, was unfamiliar with sheep. He was more used to the water buffalo that worked in the paddy fields near his grandparents. He'd never considered venturing into the field behind C Block when the sheep were in it. He didn't *think* sheep could do him much harm, but they seemed such unpredictable creatures and some had fearsome-looking horns. He decided to take no chances and approached the building in a wide arc, where there were fewer sheep. Even so a number of inquisitive sheep followed him closely.

He'd survived typhoons, deserted islands and attacks by pirates so he'd lived through far worse dangers than this, but *they* hadn't happened when he was alone in the dark!

A few metres from the building the thought crossed Lee's mind for the first time that the door might be locked! If it was, he would have no alternative but to turn and face the animals to get back to the road!

Fortunately, it was only loosely tied with hairy, white string. Once inside Lee slammed the door shut, leaving them to bleat their protests amongst themselves in the night air and struck a match. By its flickering light he could see that inside it was about the same size as his room back at the camp, though over half this building was filled up to the cobwebbed underside of the blue-grey slates by dry, sickly-sweet smelling hay.

Just before the match burnt his fingers, and he was forced to stamp it out on the earth floor, Lee noticed a rusty paraffin lamp hanging from a nail above the window. Never having expected to spend the night marooned in the dark, he hadn't thought to bring a torch. Lee shook the lamp. Some liquid sloshed about, and after a couple of tries he managed to light it and hung it back on the hook above the window, to avoid setting fire to the hay. By its pale yellow light he took in his surroundings, coming to the conclusion he could have been far worse off.

The hay would not only give him something reasonably comfortable and dry to sleep on, but added greatly to the insulation of the thin, brick walls. He drank half of his last carton of orange juice, leaving the rest for morning, hollowed out a deep nest in the hay, blew out the lamp and tried to sleep.

As he lay there in the dark, listening to the distant hum of the traffic on the motorway and the sporadic bleating from the sheep, plus an occasional curious scraping sound when they used a corner of the building as a scratching post, Lee thought of Scotty, probably asleep in his own bed by now.

So would his family be. He could predict almost exactly what they would be thinking. Kim would think he was very selfish to go off without letting her share in the secret. His mother would be upset; his father annoyed, *because* his mother was upset. Grandmother, probably not having noticed his absence, would want to know what all the fuss was about. Once it was explained to her, she would blame it all on the modern Western attitudes to bringing up children insisting that, 'None of this would have happened if Grandfather had still been alive!'

And Tam? She was the one who liked to be certain of exactly where every member of her family was. Perhaps because she was the youngest and only six when they'd left the home she could now barely remember, Tam had grown up with a constant fear of being lost, or left behind like their Uncle Loc. Throughout a life of constant moves and upheavals, many of which she didn't properly understand, Tam more than anyone had clung tightly to her family through a series of rituals. These included saying good night to each of them individually, even if it meant she had to walk round the entire camp to do it.

In Sham Shui Po they'd lived for two years in a huge aircraft hangar-like galvanised-iron building with two hundred other people, but every night Tam had scrambled up to all three levels of the triple-decker bunk that was their home to say good night to each in turn. Sometimes, if Kim had disappeared with one of her boyfriends and couldn't be found, Tam was more deeply disturbed even than Grandmother.

Lee comforted himself with the knowledge that what he was trying to do was for the benefit of the whole family but as he drifted into sleep the thought of Tam went with him into his dreams. Not as herself, but looking like a sleeping Suzie, her bedraggled doll with the torn, blue dress. Worst of all, though she had Tam's smooth, oval face, she also had the one searching, ever-open eye of the doll.

Lee woke early, stiff and cold. Daylight seeped through the grimy window although it was only five o'clock. While he ate the last of his supplies, an odd breakfast of cold chicken and some chocolate all washed down with orange juice, he thought about the terrible mistake he'd made yesterday and considered what lay ahead of him. He also pictured his family, asleep in their comfortable beds and wished he could be transported back to them on some magic carpet.

'And what would that solve?' he asked himself. 'Nothing! I'd just be back where I started, as miserable and trapped as ever. I've got to get to London and talk to Bill Keever but today's Thursday and he leaves for America tomorrow!'

With a renewed sense of urgency Lee set out across the field back towards the slip road. When he climbed the fence Lee noticed the figure of a man standing, silently watching him from the far side of the sheep field. Only when Lee had dropped down into the road did the man turn and walk away towards the farm.

Lee proved lucky and at the same time unlucky with lifts. He'd hardly put his thumb out when a farmer stopped to pick him up, but the man was only going down to the next exit and Lee's second lift of the day turned out to be equally short.

By lunch-time, having made an early start, he'd had four lifts but had failed to cover the two hundred miles he'd done with Scotty in less time the previous day. But at least his last lift dropped him at a service station, so he was able to eat and buy one or two emergency rations, though of course that meant spending money, which he was reluctant to do.

Immediately after lunch he got a lift in a two-seater white Toyota with a man returning to the Potteries from Scotland.

All morning the drivers who'd picked him up had barely spoken in the brief times he'd spent with them, though learning from his mistakes of the day before, Lee had always been careful to state clearly he was bound for London, but this man never stopped talking.

'I'm in bathrooms,' he announced proudly almost before the car had started to move.

'Please?' Lee was baffled by what sounded like a medical problem and wondered if they'd have to stop every few miles for this man to relieve himself.

'I sell bathroom suites. I thought about it long and hard before I took the job. I had a chance to go into tableware, but I thought, no! People can always struggle along with only a plate and a mug but they'll always need a bathroom. Mind you, there are still two thousand five hundred people with no piped water. But they're getting it and when they do I'll be there to sell them bathrooms!'

Realising there was no need for him to answer, Lee had begun to drift off when the man suddenly turned to him and said, 'Some cloakrooms in your Chinese restaurants leave a great deal to be desired.'

'I am Vietnamese,' Lee said quickly.

'Oh, yes? I suppose you live in that camp just outside Stoke?' Lee nodded. 'Been there about four years now, haven't you? I remember reading about it in the paper. When it first opened, they said you were only going to stay a couple of years before you moved on.'

'The camp has been open four and a half years, but very few of the people who first came are still there.'

'More have come since? Mind you, I suppose it's a bit difficult to tell really. One Vietnamese looks much like another,' the man said and laughed heartily at his own joke.

Not to another Vietnamese, Lee thought to himself, but he was too polite to say so.

'I suppose the Vietnamese have bathrooms?' the man said, but before Lee could reply he went on, 'Japanese don't believe in baths, you know? They say we sit in our own dirt. Rum idea! They pour water over their bodies and let it run straight off down the plug-hole. Wouldn't suit me, I like a good soak. Mind you, I do shower trays too.'

During the man's long monologue on the drive south Lee decided to try and make the rest of the journey to London by train. Having lost so much time by going in the wrong direction, time was passing very quickly, it was already late afternoon and if he didn't want to risk missing Bill Keever he had to get to London by evening.

He sighed impatiently. Over thirty hours later he would shortly be back one junction further north of where he'd been picked up by Scotty. What was worse, he was still dangerously close to the camp. Having been away for almost two whole days, his absence must have been reported to the Camp Director, possibly the police. People would be looking for him and they wouldn't have far to look!

By the time the salesman turned off the motorway and dropped Lee, as he'd requested, at the railway station, Lee's head was aching with the strain of listening and translating. Even when Lee was out of the car and with taxis hooting for him to move out of the way, the man wouldn't stop talking. 'I don't suppose one of our catalogues would be much good to you.'

Lee shook his head, thinking of the cold communal bathrooms back at the camp which could well do with replacing. 'Not until we get a house.'

'Oh, well, here's my card for when you do. Just give me a ring. I've got some lovely suites I could do you at a reduced price now the colour's gone out of fashion. Suit you too – they're in Bamboo!'

As he drove away the man was still laughing.

Lee felt quite overwhelmed by the Victorian splendour of the booking hall at Stoke-on-Trent railway station with its polished stone pillars, concealed lighting and potted plants. It made him think of the few French colonial buildings remaining in Saigon.

'Please, how much is a ticket to London?' he asked when his turn came but the glass of the ticket-office window was thick and he had great difficulty in hearing the reply. 'Please?'

The clerk spoke more clearly. 'When are you coming back?'

The man added something about White Saver Days and Blue Saver Days which Lee didn't understand at all. He shook his head. 'I will not be coming back by train.'

'Twenty-one pounds return is the cheapest ticket,' the clerk said.

Lee knew without counting that he hadn't enough money. 'But I don't want a return,' he protested.

The queue of travellers behind Lee was growing longer by the second. They tapped their feet, anxiously comparing their watches with the station clock.

With a shrug the clerk pointed out, 'An ordinary single ticket's dearer than that.'

Lee couldn't understand how it could possibly cost more to

go in only one direction than to make a return journey. 'Please?' he said.

'Excuse me!' the man behind Lee interrupted. 'My train leaves in two minutes, either book your ticket, or let somebody else!'

With a sigh Lee abandoned the idea of trying to reach London by train, moved away from the window and having hated drawing attention to himself, slunk out of the station.

As people rushed by Lee's head was spinning. Should he try Tran's other idea of travelling by coach but time wasn't on his side and he had no idea if he would be able to afford a ticket. Added to that, not knowing where the bus station was, he might waste valuable time on a fruitless search wandering about the unfamiliar city, misunderstanding the directions people gave him.

What was certain was that the longer he hung about, only miles from the camp, the greater the chance of somebody spotting him and whisking him back! He also knew, if that happened he would never be able to face up to explaining to Chi his monumental failure. What possible excuse could there be for travelling hundreds of miles back and forth only to end up back where he started having achieved absolutely nothing?

There was no real alternative left but to hitchhike to London. Lee carefully retraced the journey he'd made from the motorway junction with the traveller in bathrooms.

But he hadn't realised that whilst the road he was using, which was chock-full with two lanes of fast-moving commuter traffic, didn't forbid pedestrians, neither was it designed for them! There was no real pavement, only a narrow uneven grass verge. When the road dived under bridges the verge ended abruptly and Lee was forced to walk in the gutter, high-speed traffic whistling past his ear, horns blaring as they swerved to avoid him.

Fortunately, he hadn't gone far before an open-topped two-seater sports car pulled up and a pretty woman with curly brown hair ignored the hooting traffic as she called out to him. 'Trying to get yourself killed?'

'I am trying to get to the motorway.'

'Jump in,' she said with an anxious look over her shoulder, 'before somebody drives into the back of me!'

Lee climbed into the car and soon they were tearing down the fast lane.

'Where are you going?' she asked, as she skilfully weaved her car through some slow moving traffic.

'London.'

'Me too,' she smiled. 'I'll be able to take you all the way.'

Lee couldn't believe his luck! He would make it in time after all!

NINE

'So, why are you going to London ... I'm sorry, my name's Erica and you are ... ?'

'Lee.'

'Are you just going to visit friends, Lee?'

Unlike the bathroom salesman Erica didn't talk for the sake of it and they had travelled some miles down the motorway before she asked him the question. Lee had spent some of that time wondering whether he should lie to cover his tracks, but he'd decided that would be unfair when she was doing him such a great favour. Besides, she seemed a nice person with an easy smile that made her sea-green eyes flash like beacons.

'There's a man I have to see,' he began and then explained the whole purpose of his mission and that it was not only for himself he was doing this, but for the whole family.

Erica, eyes on the road and moving her car confidently through the heavy traffic, listened to his whole story in silence. After he'd finished she thought for some moments before she said, 'Lee, are you sure that America is really going to be the answer to all your problems? Apart from the fact that you might be putting England down because it's taking you so long to get a toehold here, it seems to me you might be in danger of fantasising about an America which doesn't really exist. They have unemployment too, you know, and without the kind of safety-nets we have in terms of unemployment and health care.'

Lee nodded. 'Yes, I know all that.'

'There's a terrific immigrant community already and I know it's called "The land of opportunity", but that suggests you have the chance to fail as well as succeed.'

'I realise that too, but at least we will be able to make a start and also it is for my father's sake. He sacrificed a great deal for the Americans when they were in our country and I know he feels very let down by them refusing to take him in when he was in trouble.'

'Don't you think that your obsession to get to America has blinded you to some of this country's good points?' Erica asked.

'I guess that's true,' Lee admitted.

'What it all really comes down to is Chi, isn't it?' she said quietly.

Though normally he would have avoided talking about Chi there was something about Erica which made him want to share the recent doubts he'd been having about their relationship.

'It was,' Lee said thoughtfully, 'now I'm not so sure.'

Erica smiled. 'I know it's a very long time since you last saw each other but judging by the way you spoke about her just now nothing can have changed.'

Choosing his words very carefully, Lee told Erica about Warren.

'Does she mention him by name in her letters?'

'No, not for ages, that is what makes me so suspicious!'

Erica laughed out loud. 'We do torture ourselves sometimes.' Then her voice grew serious. 'Lee, you must be very careful. Jealousy can be a very destructive emotion. I was once in love with somebody. I thought he was so wonderful that I couldn't believe every other woman in the world wouldn't want him too. That was okay in itself, until I convinced myself that they were out to get him.'

'Was he unfaithful to you?'

'I thought so.'

'What did you do?'

'At first silly things like check his diary, to see who he was meeting. But it began to get worse. I started to search his pockets for clues, restaurant bills, that sort of thing and I was always going through his things trying to find presents he might have been given.'

'Did you find anything?'

'Nothing, but still I wasn't convinced. I decided to confront him and although he laughed and said I was the only one he loved, I didn't believe him. Things got worse between us because of my constant questioning of his every move until we were hardly on speaking terms. I was so stupid, I believed it was his guilt that was making everything so awful. Things came to a head one night when I hid outside his office and followed him to a pub where he met this astonishingly beautiful woman. I wanted to scratch her eyes out! Trouble was, I tried! I went into the pub and there was a terrible scene.'

'I think I might do the same thing if I found Chi with Warren.'

'Well, take my tip, don't do it. Not until you know *all* the facts. It turned out this woman genuinely was a business contact for a deal worth thousands of pounds which I succeeded in fouling up completely. Business hadn't been going too well for him anyway, another reason why he'd been acting a bit strange, and this finished him off. We split up soon after that and it was all my fault. Lee, jealousy usually says more about ourselves and our insecurities than about other people and it's like an acid, it eats things away but often does it so slowly you don't realise what's happening until there's nothing left.'

'In her last letter, Chi said, "Things work themselves out in the end".'

Erica nodded. 'I think Chi's right. You've got to remember she's living in a foreign country where there's an awful lot of new things for her to tackle and a heavy emphasis on success. She needs all the help she can get, even if some of that comes from a man. And while it's quite possible that Warren may have other ideas, if Chi's really like you say she is, she'll have told him exactly where she stands.'

'You think she will have told Warren about me?'

'Believe me, I bet he's sick of the sound of your name by now!'

Feeling much better for Erica's reassurances, Lee settled back and enjoyed the rest of the drive, though for him, eagerly looking forward to seeing Bill Keever again, it couldn't go quickly enough.

It was after seven when Erica dropped him in Grosvenor Square, right at the foot of the steps to the floodlit front of the United States embassy. As Lee climbed out of the car Erica leant across. 'Lee, I hope everything works out for you, especially with Chi. I think she's a really lucky girl to be loved so much by someone like you.'

Lee blushed, thanked her for the lift and watched the tail lights of her car disappear into the gathering dusk. His stomach bubbled with excitement as he gazed up to where the floodlit, gold American eagle perched protectively above the huge, solid-looking building. He experienced a sense of relief. Despite all his mistakes his journey was over at long last and, if his meeting with Bill went well, he'd probably be back at the camp tomorrow and soon the whole family would be on the last lap of their journey, too.

So sure was the feeling of his mission being almost over, that the moment he was inside the embassy doors Lee felt he had at least one foot already on American soil and was rather surprised to be confronted by an English security man though the epaulets on his white shirt said Pinkerton's Securities. 'Name?' he asked.

'Mr Keever,' Lee replied.

The man sighed. 'You're Mr Keever?'

'No, I'm Lee Nguyen. I want to see ... '

The man held up his hand like a traffic policeman to stop Lee while he put on gold-rimmed glasses and laboriously wrote Lee's name into a book, efficiently checking his watch so that he could enter the arrival time. Only when he'd finished did he look up again. 'Now, young fella, what can we do for you?'

'I want to talk to Mr Keever, Mr Bill Keever.'

'Do you now?' The man checked through some typewritten lists on a clipboard. 'Well, it's *Senator* Keever for a start,' he said, laying heavy emphasis on the title.

Though Lee wasn't certain exactly what a senator was, except that he was something important to do with the government, Lee was very impressed. 'He did say he was a guest of the ambassador's, but I did not know he was a senator!'

'Well, now you do. And is Senator Keever expecting you?'

The first pangs of unease made Lee shift from foot to foot. 'No, he isn't,' he admitted but added brightly, 'though I'm sure he'll see me when he knows I'm here. We played tennis together.'

'High circles you do mix in, I must say.'

'And I beat him!' Lee added proudly.

The man looked disbelievingly down over his glasses at Lee as he picked up a phone. 'Mmm. Well, let's see if the gentleman's in first, shall we, before we decide about a re-match?' He punched out a number. 'I'm sorry to trouble you,' he said into the phone, 'but I've got a young man here who hasn't got an appointment, but says he'd like a word with Senator Keever.' There was a pause while the man listened to a voice on the other end of the line. 'Yes, yes, I see. Thank you and I am sorry to trouble you.' He replaced the telephone and turned back to Lee. 'Well, young fella, it seems you're out of luck. Senator Keever isn't staying here though he is here with the ambassador tonight. Under no circumstances can he be disturbed.'

Lee couldn't believe what he was hearing. 'But I've got to see him,' he protested.

'Not tonight you can't,' the man said firmly.

'But I've come a long way, it's very important and he goes back to America tomorrow!'

The man shook his head. 'That's as maybe, but, you see, your mistake was not making an appointment. Should have made an appointment.'

'What can I do?'

'You could ring up for one tomorrow,' the man suggested. 'Or come back again on the off chance that he's free. He's coming in early.' Seeing how miserably deflated Lee was, he added, 'Sorry, son, but that's the way it is.'

Lee stood at the top of the steps outside the embassy. Although it was dark apart from the streetlights, birds were still squabbling noisily over roosting spaces amongst the trees in the square. He knew how they felt – where was he going to spend the night? He had always assumed he'd talk to Bill Keever and get a lift home. Now here he was, with Bill about to leave the next day, marooned in a strange city with nowhere to sleep and not enough money to pay for anywhere.

The loud rumbling of his stomach made his first decision for him, reminding him that he hadn't eaten since lunch-time and the first thing he must do was get something to eat.

Having no idea which way to go, Lee wandered to the end of the square and seeing a stream of traffic at the end of the road, set out towards it. It wasn't, he quickly discovered, a good choice. The broad road he emerged on, Park Lane, was full of large, expensive-looking hotels with uniformed doormen who either gave him suspicious looks as he approached, or ignored him. Luckily, walking against the stream of traffic, he soon found himself amongst the bright lights of Marble Arch where he had no difficulty finding a fast-food shop.

While he hungrily tucked into a monster burger with everything, he thought about his next move. The hay-filled hut where he'd spent the previous night hadn't seemed much at the time but he knew he'd be lucky to find anything as comfortable tonight!

He remembered Tran talking about the Vietnamese who ran a restaurant in Swiss Cottage, but he had no idea of its name, or even where Swiss Cottage was, so he decided that was hopeless. He could try to find the headquarters of the Morning Star Battalion in Wimbledon. It was just possible that they'd take pity on him and give him a bed for the night, but again, without the address, the chances of finding somewhere like that were pretty remote. There were also the Vietnamese Tran had visited, who'd been rehoused in London. If only he'd thought about the possibility of having to stay the night he could have got their address from Tran. He briefly considered the idea of ringing Tran at the camp but instantly dismissed it. He didn't want to give away his whereabouts, at least not until after he'd seen Bill Keever.

His meal finished, Lee wandered out on to the street. It was only half-past nine. To find some form of shelter and to pass the time, Lee wandered along Oxford Street, stopping occasionally to gaze in at the brightly lit shop-window displays. One, which featured half a dozen comfortable-looking beds, particularly appealed to him and if wishes had worked he would have passed straight through the glass to spend the night on one of those!

A stroll down Regent Street brought him into Piccadilly, where he noticed people rushing down the steps towards the Underground and followed them. Though he knew nothing of London's Underground he was familiar with a similar system, the Mass Transit, in Hong Kong. He studied the wall-map with its different coloured routes. He noticed the station at

Heathrow, the airport where he'd first arrived in England, and also found both Swiss Cottage and Wimbledon but knew it was useless going out to them. With only one day left the closer he stayed to the American embassy the better. He was frightened of losing his way back and he wanted to be certain of being there first thing in the morning.

Still worried about finding somewhere to spend the night, Lee joined the crowd of people hurrying up Shaftesbury Avenue past the artists who were crouched on stools drawing tourists' portraits.

One thing he noticed and enjoyed about wandering through the streets of London was that he no longer stood out from the crowd. Unlike the small town near the camp in the Midlands, London's streets seemed to be full of every imaginable race. Even the snatches of conversations he overheard were in a multitude of different languages and he felt far more comfortable than he had since he first arrived in England.

When it started to rain Lee dodged into a smoke-filled amusement arcade packed with people of about his own age. Some were fiercely concentrating on noisy buzzing, bleeping computer games as they drove round complex racing tracks, or attempted to destroy enemy spacecraft.

All were watched over with an air of deep suspicion verging on loathing by a thin man with a pot belly, narrow eyes and greasy black hair, who sat under a sign saying 'Change Given'.

A hoarse voice piped up beside Lee. 'You goin' to play the machines?'

Lee turned to find a thin boy of about twelve standing next to him. He was dressed in a grubby denim jacket, slashed drainpipe jeans and Doc Martens. His tee-shirt had the words "YOU PICKED THE WRONG ONE" on it. He had a pale pink face and red hair, cut very short, which made his red ears appear to stick out like the handles on one of the tennis cups Lee had won.

'You goin' to play?' the boy repeated when Lee didn't immediately answer.

Lee shook his head. 'I have never used one.'

'I'll show you. Got fifty p?'

'Yes, but ... '

'Oh, it's no trouble,' the boy said. 'I don't mind showin' you.'

Knowing he was being conned, Lee reluctantly handed over a coin which the red-head inserted into the machine. Lee noticed the boy had the letters L-O-V-E M-U-M tattooed on the middle joint of his fingers.

When the machine failed to start the boy thumped it very hard, first with L-O-V-E and then with M-U-M.

The man behind the change desk broke off from handing over coins to shout at him. 'Hey, you! Knock it orf! That's a 'ighly sophisticated piece of state-of-the-art equipment, not a punchbag!'

'Yes, well, it's just nicked my fifty p!'

Lee thought the boy had got a cheek considering it was *his* money!

The man's eyes narrowed to slits. 'I bet you've been stuffing it with washers again.'

'I haven't!' the red-head said, pale green eyes wide with innocence.

The man reluctantly locked the cash drawer, hauled himself up and slouched across with a huge set of keys on a thick chrome chain with which he unlocked the faulty machine. After he'd poked about unsuccessfully amongst its innards for a few seconds, he locked it up and gave it a vicious, glancing blow on the side with the open palm of his grimy hand, as if he was cuffing its ear! Instantly the machine sprang into action.

'That's all I was doin'!' the boy protested.

'Yeah,' the man said, looking at him as if nothing would have given him greater pleasure than to give the boy's red head the same treatment, 'but I'm a hexpert, aren't I? I'm paid to know *where* to 'it them. Now clear orf!'

'But my fifty p!'

'Hop it, the both of you.'

'I don't even know him,' Lee said.

But the man wasn't interested in explanations. 'You 'eard me – out.'

'That's stealin'!' the boy said.

'No, it isn't,' the man replied with a leer, pointing up at a blue sign just above his head which said, in gold lettering, "The Management retain the right to refuse admission". 'Both of you, out!'

'That's a rip off!' the boy said bravely, but when "The Management" took a step towards him, ominously swinging the heavy bunch of keys round in front of him like an aeroplane propeller, the boy grabbed Lee's arm and pulled him towards the door in a hasty retreat.

The boy shouted back over his shoulder, 'I'm never comin' back here again.'

'And that'll be too soon!' the man said scornfully.

It was still raining. Pedestrians caught in the heavy shower were covering their heads with umbrellas as they scurried for the Underground or queued for buses. Lee zipped up his anorak. The boy turned up his collar, stuck his hands in his pockets and began to lope off along the street. He paused briefly to glance back at Lee. 'You comin' or what?'

Lee shrugged and ran to catch him up. After all, he didn't have anything else pressing to do, yet, or anywhere special to go. In fact without the boy he would be lost.

TEN

'I haven't seen you around before,' the red-head muttered as he loped along, keeping up a steady pace as if he had urgent business to attend to. 'You just got here?'

'Yes.'

'Run away from home?'

'Sort of, but I am going back.'

'Yes, that's what I said. Just come for a look round "but I am going back"!' he mimicked Lee. 'That was eight months ago. There's no way I'm going back now. Not while *he's* still there!' Lee was about to ask who "he" was but the boy grabbed his arm and dragged him down a side street.

'What did you do that for?' Lee asked as they took another sharp turn up a darkened alley.

'Fuzz! Didn't you see them?'

'Fuzz?'

'Pigs, coppers. Don't you understand English? Police!'

'Oh, I see, but we haven't done anything wrong.'

'Maybe we haven't, but if they clap eyes on us they'll whistle us straight back home quicker than you can blink. They call me Red, what's your name?'

'Lee.'

'You Chinese or somethin'?'

'Vietnamese.'

'You hungry?' Red didn't wait for an answer. 'Me, I'm starvin'.' He set off with a determined air while Lee tagged along behind. Lee was wondering, if Red had enough money to buy food, why Red had bothered to con him out of money for the slot machine. The explanation wasn't long in coming.

Red led them out on to another crowded street and tried to stop people by using in his hoarse, plaintive voice, a variety of phrases which all carried a similar message.

'Got somethin' for a cup of tea?' 'My mum's gone off and left me.' 'Spare 50p.'

Lee felt very embarrassed about the idea of begging. He considered leaving Red to it, but he guessed that somebody who'd been on the run for eight months and knew his way round the streets, must know of somewhere to sleep. He decided his chances were better with Red.

'Aren't you goin' to help?' Red demanded.

Lee's answer was to creep back into a shop doorway while Red begged for money with a desolate expression on his face and a method of palming the few coins given to him that was worthy of any conjurer.

Women seemed more vulnerable to Red's waif-like charm but when a man walked straight up to Red and said something very quietly into the boy's ear, Red's expression changed quickly to one of red-faced anger.

'Read my tee-shirt!' he shouted, flashing the words "YOU PICKED THE WRONG ONE". 'I'll get the police to you, you dirty old man,' he called after the hastily departing man. Then, to Lee's astonishment Red burst into noisy tears.

A group of women quickly gathered to comfort him.

'I do need a bed for the night,' Red howled to them, 'but not that bad!'

They offered him Kleenex tissues to dry his eyes and Lee saw several coins handed over before Red eventually calmed down and shook the women off.

'Lee, I think we've cracked it!' Red said proudly, leading the way into the nearest hamburger bar.

They were hardly through the door when a neatly-dressed waitress with piled-up grey hair rushed across to block their path. 'You've been told before, you're not to come in here begging, you little terror!'

Lee started to make for the door as the entire restaurant went silent and all the diners turned to stare at them.

But Red held his ground defiantly. 'Is that any way to talk to a payin' customer?' he said in an injured tone, holding out a handful of coins for the waitress to see. 'Money earned, I might say, by the sweat of honest toil.'

'Aye,' the waitress said sarcastically, 'that'll be the day!'

'Do we get served, or do we have to take our custom

elsewhere?' Red demanded cockily.

'You cheeky monkey!' The waitress looked as if she was about to cuff Red round his red ears but, just in time, she realised the customers had changed sides and were now laughing at the boy's impudence. With an impatient gesture she waved them towards a table on its own. 'You'd best sit over there, where at least the customers won't have to put up with the smell of you! And keep well away from that coat-rack!'

'What does she mean?' Lee whispered.

'Search me!' Red said innocently. 'Maybe she thinks I need a new jacket and I might help myself. As if I'd do a thing like that!'

Whatever the truth, while they ate their hamburgers which the waitress insisted Red paid for on delivery, Lee couldn't help noticing, as the heat of the restaurant slowly began to dry out their clothes, that Red did give off a rather curious stale smell!

'Still raining!' Red said as he noisily sucked up the dregs of the banana milk shake through his straw. 'I know what, we'll go and see a film.'

Before Lee could protest that he didn't want to waste the money, Red was up and by the door, calling back to the waitress, "Bye, Mum, see you when you get home!"

After that Lee had no choice but to follow! 'Where are we going?'

'There's a place up the road, always has a late show.'

'I haven't any money,' Lee lied.

'I'll get you in.'

Thinking Red was offering to pay for him, Lee suggested it might be better if he kept his money for the next time he was hungry.

'Plenty more where that came from,' Red called out over his shoulder as he trotted through the rain, making sure he stamped his boots hard into every black puddle, much to the annoyance of the other pedestrians who got splattered.

'But what's the film?' Lee asked jogging beside him.

Red gave him a pitying look. 'What difference does that make? It'll be warm and dry, won't it?'

They stopped outside the cinema and Red started searching

through a packed litter-bin.

'What are you doing?' Lee asked.

'Need a drinks can.'

'There's one in the gutter over there.' Lee pointed at an empty Coke tin. 'What's that for?'

'Our entrance ticket,' Red said as he picked up the can. 'Be ready when I tell you.'

Totally baffled, Lee watched in amazement as Red slowly and carefully opened the swing door just wide enough to get his arm and the can through. Then he lobbed the Coke can into a corner of the foyer where it fell with a loud clatter and then rolled noisily across the stone floor.

A man shot out of the ticket office in the direction of the sound of the can. 'Who's that? What's going on?'

'Now!' Red hissed and dragged Lee across the foyer in the opposite direction until they were in the darkened cinema. Red instantly dropped to his knees, indicating Lee should do the same and began to crawl quickly along an empty row of seats amongst the sweet wrappers, sticky ice-cream cartons and empty popcorn packets.

Lee stopped moving and breathing when he heard the man's voice behind him saying, in an angry whisper, 'I'll find you, don't think I won't!'

Several people watching the film turned round to shush him but the man wasn't easily put off. Lee crouched in a tight ball as the torch beam swept round the cinema. It reminded Lee of hiding in their boat while it was still in the estuary and a Vietnamese gunboat had pulled alongside, sweeping its searchlight across them.

But the man was forced to abandon the search due to the protests of the paying customers when his torch-beam still hadn't found the two boys.

'Look what I got,' Red said as he flopped down in a seat, 'half a packet of peanuts somebody's dropped! Must be one of me good days! Want some?'

Lee shook his head. Sitting next to Red watching the film, a very slow story about peasants being moved off their land, Lee was getting quite worried about what they'd been doing.

Although he couldn't help admiring Red's cheek and ingenuity, the boy was obviously not the most honest person in the world and Lee had a distinct feeling that any minute he might get them both into real trouble. Lee didn't fancy ending up in a police station. Especially if that meant, as Red had suggested earlier, being sent straight back to the camp before he'd had a chance to talk to Bill Keever. The only reason Lee had stuck with Red was because he needed somewhere to sleep and he decided it was time he found out if Red could supply the answer. If he couldn't, he'd be safer on his own!

'Where do you sleep?' Lee whispered.

'All sorts of places. Down the Underground.'

'Don't they lock it up at night?'

'Sure, but you go down last thing. There are plenty of places to hide. Then there's warm grilles round the back of hotels. They're getting a bit difficult lately,' Red admitted. 'The posh people, who've just spent a hundred pounds on a meal, don't like comin' face to face with us down and outs. Turns their stomachs, or consciences, or somethin'. I used to sleep in the railway carriages in the railway sidings outside Euston until one mornin' I got woken up in Warrington by a bolshie ticket inspector!'

'So where do you sleep now?'

'If it's dry I usually sleep out in one of the squares.'

'But it's raining tonight.'

'Yes, we'd best go down Waterloo way. There's a couple of good places down there.'

They nearly spent the night in the cinema! By the time the long, boring film had dragged to a close they were both fast asleep and only the banging of seats, as the other people left, woke them.

'Split up and hide among the crowd so the bloke doesn't see us,' Red hissed at Lee as they walked up the aisle towards the foyer. His caution paid off. Lee noticed that the man with the torch, who'd chased them into the cinema, was searching the small crowd leaving, craning his neck to see if he could spot the people who'd got in without paying.

Lee, feeling very unhappy, managed to hide on the other side

101

of a large woman in a pink coat, but his politeness let him down! When Lee stood back to hold open the glass swing door, for the woman to pass through first, the man recognised him and jumped forward with a shout. 'Hey, you! Come back here.' For a second Lee froze.

'Run!' shouted Red, who was already waiting for him on the pavement.

As the man's hand came down to grab Lee's anorak Lee sprang into life, but not before the man had caught hold of him by the hood. 'Got you!' the man said grimly.

But Lee knew better! He surged forward, press-studs popped and Lee shot into the street like a cork from a bottle, leaving the man shouting and looking rather foolish holding the detachable hood.

'Nice one!' Red said as they jogged through the streets until they had put a safe distance between them and the cinema. As they slowed down to a walk Red said, half under his breath, 'Sometimes I get sick of running!'

It was the first time Lee had seen any crack in Red's armour but, as they set out on the long walk to Waterloo, it made him wonder just how much of the boy's cocky air of independence was really only a front.

It was one o'clock in the morning. The rain had eased to a steady, incessant drizzle that soaked them both through. By the time they reached Charing Cross any warmth and comfort they'd gained from the cinema had been long forgotten. Red's hair was plastered to his head and Lee's teeth were chattering.

When they dodged under an arch off Villiers Street Lee hoped that at last they had found some shelter but Red shook his head. 'Can't sleep here,' he said firmly.

'Why not?'

'It's all drunks and winos here. Look around you.'

Lee looked. The arch was in fact a long tunnel, open at both ends and lit by occasional hanging lights, that ran beneath Charing Cross station.

In the pale pools of light Lee could see shadowy figures spread throughout the length of the tunnel. Some had fallen down in the middle of the pavement and slept where they lay, muttering and twitching in their sleep. Others sat hunched against the wall staring wide-eyed and unseeing in front of them as they took regular swigs from the bottles they gripped by the neck.

Two men, who had their arms round each other's necks, bottles in their free hands, twirled round and round in a slow, unsteady, drunken dance, singing at the tops of their voices. The words, which were unintelligible, echoed eerily round the curved walls of the tunnel. One of the dancing drunks accidentally stepped on the hand of a sleeping body. The body, a short thick-set man with a shock of grey hair, who was swathed in an old RAF greatcoat, woke up with a scream and hurled his empty bottle at the drunks. It missed them completely but he had already passed out before his bottle hit the wall and smashed into fragments.

'It's no good stoppin' here anyway, 'cos the fuzz keeps coming round all night movin' you on. You never get a wink of sleep here. Hey, grab those newspapers!' Red said, nudging the appalled Lee back to life.

'But there's somebody asleep under them.'

'He's too drunk to know the difference!' Red said scornfully, snatching them up for him. 'Look, if you're so choosy, there's a cardboard box over there, we could use a couple of those.'

Further down the street Red whooped with delight when he found another enormous box lined with polystyrene foam packing. 'Don't half keep you warm, that does!' he said, struggling to carry the box which was nearly as big as he was.

Carrying their prizes, together with a few more newspapers they found by a newsstand and stuffed into the boxes to keep them dry, they crossed the Thames by a footbridge. They wandered through the South Bank complex of darkened concrete and glass. Only a few hours earlier it had been lively with theatre and concertgoers but now it was deserted.

Once across the main road they dived down a subway and began to pass through sleeping figures lying against the walls.

'Although it's quieter, this doesn't seem much better than the other place,' Lee said quietly.

'Ah,' Red said knowingly, 'but here you get a better class of down and out! Less drunks and drug addicts.'

Lee jumped as a head popped out from a bundle of what looked like old clothes right by his feet. 'Hi, Red,' the young man said, 'you're late. You missed the kitchen.'

'Kitchen?' said Lee.

'Soup kitchen, comes round here every night. Oh, well never mind.'

'It's all right, I said you'd be here and I kept you a pie and some soup,' the man said and reaching down under his bundle, he produced a plastic cup of soup with a lid on it and a pie wrapped in paper. 'Sorry, mate, didn't know you were coming,' he apologised to Lee.

'That is okay,' Lee smiled.

'He can share mine,' Red offered. 'Good night.'

'Good night,' the man said and popped his head back under the bundle of clothes like a tortoise going back in its shell.

'That's what I mean about meetin' a better class of person down here,' Red said with pride. 'That bloke's holdin' down a job and he's only sleepin' down here while he saves up the deposit for a room. Look, this should do us.' They put the boxes down against the wall. 'I'm all in,' Red admitted. 'Why don't we eat this and then we'll turn in.'

Red tore the meat and potato pie in half. It was lukewarm but very welcome, as was the onion soup which they passed back and forth between them.

Between mouthfuls Lee, who'd been looking bleary-eyed at the sleeping figures that lined the subway, said, 'Red, how long are you going to live like this?'

Red shrugged.

'Why don't you go home?'

'Not while *he's* there,' Red said with the same bitterness he'd used before.

'Who is *he*?'

Red glared at the wall opposite. 'Bloke moved in with my mum. She said I should call him uncle, but I won't call him anything – except bastard! 'Cos that's what he is! He never liked me. Thumped me from morning to breakfast, he did.'

'Why does your mother put up with him?'

'Oh, he's nice as pie to her, and me, until her back's turned.

104

Then he starts in on me again.' Red angrily pulled his tee-shirt up and revealed three ugly purple scars. 'He did that! He swiped me over and over again with a length of wire.'

'What did your mother say about that?'

'He told her I'd done it when I ran into a fence and she believed him! But I'll get him one day, when I'm bigger! Come on,' Red said, abruptly ending the conversation, 'we can't sit around talking all night, let's get the beds sorted. You have the big box.'

'No,' Lee protested, 'you found it. It is only fair you should have that.'

'Don't be daft. You'll feel the cold more than me. You'd best have it.'

Red wrapped himself in newspaper and took off his jacket which, although it was still damp, he rolled up and used as a pillow.

Lee was able to turn his anorak inside out, where it was dry and quite warm for his head, and the box, though a bit squeaky when he moved against the plastic foam, was large enough for him to curl up inside.

'Tear one of the flaps off though,' Red warned him.

'But they keep the draught out.'

'Yes, but if some silly bugger sets fire to it you can die from the fumes of the burning foam in seconds.'

'Who would set fire to it?' Lee asked, horrified.

'You'd be surprised! It's funny how some blokes get their kicks. Mate of mine got burnt alive near Poplar one night. Bunch of lager louts just did it for a laugh!'

Lee lay awake a long time after that, listening for approaching footsteps but all he heard was the distant rumble of traffic. He thought about his meeting with Bill Keever later that morning and about going home to his family.

'Funny,' he thought to himself as he tried to get comfortable, 'I never thought I'd be glad to see that camp again!'

He thought Red was asleep until the boy coughed and turned restlessly, rustling the newspapers. 'Red, don't you miss your mother?' Lee asked quietly.

Red didn't answer.

ELEVEN

At seven, having lain awake for half the night, for fear he would not wake in time, the sudden echoing footsteps of early commuters scurrying through the subway towards the City, brought Lee violently out of a particularly deep patch of sleep.

Once awake he couldn't lie still for a second. Lee's head was instantly buzzing with excitement at the thought of meeting Bill. The possibility of persuading him to sponsor them so that they could go to America and, above all, seeing Chi again.

Red was still snoring heavily until Lee disturbed him with the noise he made, uncurling himself from the cardboard.

'What's up?' Red asked, half-opening his eyes against the light.

'I have got to go,' Lee said, shivering from excitement and the cold morning air that blew through the subway. 'There's a man I must see. It's very important.'

Red sat cross-legged on the floor rubbing warmth and life back into his stiffened limbs. 'You look a bit rough for an important meetin'.'

Lee glanced down at his creased clothes and at the same time realised it was three days since he'd had a wash, let alone a shower. No wonder Red, who had lived like this for months, smelled a bit stale! 'What else can I do?'

'Come on, I'll show you.' Red hauled himself up and led Lee back across the road and up the main steps into Waterloo station.

They crossed the concourse and dived down a narrow flight of steps until Red paused outside a door marked 'PRIVATE. STAFF ONLY'. He eased the door open a crack and peered inside before he nodded for Lee to follow him.

'We should not be in here!' Lee hissed.

'You don't want to go and meet this bloke smelling like a dosser, do you?' Red whispered fiercely.

Lee had no idea what a dosser was but he was anxious

to get cleaned up before his meeting with Bill Keever, so he followed.

'Where are you seeing your bloke?' Red asked as they washed and then dried themselves on the roller towel.

'The American embassy in Grosvenor Square,' Lee replied, then froze as he remembered the long rambling route they'd taken the previous night and knew he would never be able to find his way back. 'Will you show me the way?'

'Sure!'

By the time Lee had combed his hair and got a small toothbrush and paste from a slot machine to clean his teeth he was beginning to feel much better but it was already eight and he was anxious to be off.

'Just one more thing,' Red said putting a coin into another wall-mounted slot machine. He put one hand under the nozzle and pressed a button. The washroom was filled with odour of cheap after-shave.

'But you don't shave!' Lee laughed as Red splashed it round his face.

'No, but it don't half make you feel posh! Want some?'

As Lee shook his head the washroom door was flung open and was filled by the bulk of a driver who stopped short at the sight of the two boys. 'What you doin' in 'ere? This is the drivers' washroom.'

Red wasn't fazed. 'Yes, I know. My dad said it would be all right.'

'Who's your dad?' the man demanded.

'He's takin' the eight-fifteen out to Esher.'

'Oh, I see.' The man let them pass, but just as they were going through the outer door he shouted after them. 'Hey, there's no eight-fifteen to Esher! Come back here, you two!' But the boys were already running up the steps and out of sight.

As they walked across the concourse past a newsagent's, Lee's eye was caught by a newspaper folded in half in a rack which hung on the wall outside. He stopped in his tracks. He'd found himself staring at his own photograph. Above it was the bold, black headline "**POLICE HUNT BOY**".

His parents, or the camp authorities, had obviously reported him missing and somehow the newspaper must have got hold of a copy of his camp identity photograph.

It had been taken the day they arrived and Lee remembered how annoyed his father had been at the time. 'I feel like a criminal!' he'd said, standing in front of a white sheet, holding up a small black card bearing a hastily-scrawled chalk number.

Lee desperately wanted to snatch the folded paper from the rack to read the article, but didn't want to draw attention to himself.

'You seen a ghost, or somethin'?' Red asked.

'It's nothing,' Lee said, grabbing Red's arm and propelling him away from the newsagent's. 'We've got to get a move on!'

As they passed a phone box Lee thought about ringing his parents at the camp to tell them he was all right but decided that would best be done *after* he'd talked to Bill Keever.

In the end, mainly because Red insisted on dropping in at a shelter kitchen for the homeless to pick up coffee and a hunk of bread, it was half-past nine by the time they walked into Grosvenor Square and far later than Lee had intended.

'Thank you for your help,' he said politely to Red.

'You'll be all right now then?' Red said.

'Yes, fine, thank you.' Lee was anxious to bound up the steps but Red seemed reluctant to leave. 'I have to go,' Lee said firmly.

'Yes, sure. I know that! Don't worry about me, I'll be okay. I got things to do, people to see, too, you know!'

Lee ran up the steps but when he reached the top and turned to look Red was still standing at the bottom. Lee waved a hand and called back to Red, 'I hope it all works out for you.'

Red didn't answer. He just nodded, turned, and walked off but Lee couldn't help noticing that Red seemed to have lost some of the cockiness from his stride.

The security man recognised Lee the moment he arrived at the desk. 'You just missed Senator Keever.'

Lee felt suddenly dashed. He knew he should have arrived earlier. 'Oh, no!'

'Yes,' the man said, checking his clipboard. 'He was here early but he left here at nine-seventeen.'

'Perhaps I could do what you said last night, make an appointment.'

The man shook his head. 'No good, son. He had a suitcase with him. I don't think he'll be coming back again.'

Lee was getting desperate. 'Do you know where he went?'

The man scratched his chin. 'I'm not sure I should give out that kind of information.'

'Oh, please! I have to see him, it is *very* important!'

Reluctantly the man glanced back at the clipboard. 'Well, all I know is, a taxi called for him at quarter-past nine and the driver said he was to take Senator Keever to the Albert Hall.'

Lee remembered Bill saying that was where the conference was being held, but he had no idea where it was. If only Red hadn't gone, he'd have known. 'How can I get there?'

'No problem! Walk out of here, down the side of the building until you get to the end of the street then you'll see Hyde Park opposite. Keep on the left edge of the park and you'll eventually come to the Albert Hall. Anyone'll tell you, you can't miss it. Big round domed building.'

Lee, not wishing to make any more mistakes, carefully repeated the directions and the man nodded. 'Thank you very much,' Lee said as he turned to leave.

'Just a minute, young fella.' The security man peered through his glasses at Lee. 'Wasn't it you I saw on this morning's TV news?'

Lee had instant visions of him ringing the police and knew if that happened he would never get anywhere near Bill. 'Me?' he said, trying to use the innocent tone he'd picked up from Red. 'I do not think it could have been me.'

'Something about a boy run away from home. I must admit I wasn't listening properly, the dog was barking his head off, but I could have sworn it was you.'

His palms sticky with sweat, Lee edged towards the door. 'I'm sure it wasn't me.' Then the bathroom salesman's words came back into his head. 'We Vietnamese do look very alike to Europeans.'

'Yes, I suppose,' the man said doubtfully but Lee was

through the door and gone before he could ask any more awkward questions.

Hyde Park, which proved as easy to find as the security man had suggested, came as something of a shock to Lee. Having spent hours wandering round the crowded London streets it was a very curious experience to find himself suddenly in this oasis of trees and grass. Had it been any other occasion he would have enjoyed nothing more than a quiet stroll, watching the horse riders on Rotten Row and the boats drifting idly across the Serpentine. Instead, with the constant, nagging feeling that time was running out on him, he jogged most of the way, pausing only to check with friendly-looking people that he was indeed still heading in the right direction.

Hot and breathless he sat for a few moments on the steps of the Albert Memorial. All the way through the park he'd been thinking about how to get a message to Bill. He assumed, rather like the embassy, that there would be somebody at the door he could ask. Though now he knew his face had appeared not only in at least one newspaper but on television, too, he would have to be more careful about who he talked to.

Finding a doorman in a circular building wasn't as easy as he'd expected. He'd walked three times round the outside of the building before he found the door to the foyer.

An old man with a bucket and mop was busy washing down the steps. 'You can't come in here, there's a conference going on,' the man said, blocking Lee's path.

'I know,' Lee said, 'but there's somebody in there I must talk to.'

'Sorry about that. You'll have to go round the back.'

'It is difficult to tell the front from the back of this building.'

'I know,' the old man said, gloomily. 'Look for a sign that says Stage Door.'

Lee did as he was told and went twice more round the building. He was looking so hard at all the hundreds of doors that he hadn't noticed the sign was hanging above his head.

The doorkeeper, whose cubbyhole was just inside, wasn't much help. 'No, I can't give anyone a message. Strict instructions. Nobody goes into the hall while the conference is in session. I've been telling the press that all week.'

'But do you know if Senator Keever is in there?'

'Haven't a clue. Apart from the audience there's about a hundred people on the platform. I can hardly tell one from another, that's why they have to have passes. My job is to look at their passes. I don't have time to remember names with a hundred people going through in the space of a few minutes. It's the same when them orchestras are here. I can't tell me alto from me oboe! You'll just have to be patient and wait outside until they come out.'

'When will it end?'

'About five.'

'Thank you.'

'Mind you, some of them do slip off early.'

'Right, I'll wait outside.'

'You do that, but mind you don't get knocked down in the rush,' the man warned him.

Lee hadn't dared to leave the building all day in case Bill was one of the ones who decided to leave early. Nor could he watch both front and back doors at the same time and he had been forced to patrol anxiously back and forth round the curve of the building, fearing that the moment he turned his back would be the very moment Bill would choose to leave.

All the excitement and anticipation he had felt on waking had long since disappeared and it turned out to be one of the longest days of his life. Doing nothing, yet being constantly alert on a knife edge of anticipation.

Fortunately a hot-dog stall turned up just before lunch for the benefit of the tourists, otherwise he would have had no food all day.

At about one o'clock his spirits soared as he saw people pouring out of the main door. Lee raced round to the Stage Door but the man soon put him right.

'That's just the audience going out for their sandwiches.'

'What about the others – will they eat?'

'Oh, yes. Having a buffet lunch upstairs.'

'Couldn't I go in and see Senator Keever now? Surely lunch is not private.'

'I'm not telling you again.' The man looked cross. 'No pass, no entry. Clear off before I call the police!'

The police, now that his absence had been reported to them, were the very last people Lee wanted to meet. He had managed to avoid them whilst crossing the park and he had disappeared round the building every time he saw a police car, he didn't want to ruin his chances now by upsetting the doorkeeper.

At two the people eating their packets of sandwiches in the sunshine on the steps of the Albert Memorial began to file slowly back into the auditorium.

It occurred to Lee that if he mingled with the crowd nobody would notice him and once in the auditorium if he got near enough to the front he might be able to catch Bill's eye. It was worth a try. Anything was better than hanging around waiting.

He was inside the main door and halfway across the foyer before he realised that all the people going back in were having their tickets checked.

Sandwiched between two large men and with a solid queue building up behind him it wasn't that he'd decided to risk it, more a question of being swept along by the press of people around him.

As Lee looked up he saw the velvet pelmet above the doorway was getting closer. The two men were still shielding him from the ushers' view as they checked tickets. Above and beyond the heads of the people in front Lee could already see the high, curved ceiling of the hall. Two more steps and he'd be there!

He held his breath as he passed under the velvet pelmet.

One more step!

'Is that young man with either of you gentlemen?'

Both men turned and looked down in astonishment at Lee, then shook their heads.

An usher's hand made a grab at Lee. For a split second he wondered whether to make a dash for it, into the auditorium.

But this was not like the darkened cinema where he'd been able to hide between the seats. The auditorium was brightly lit and being chased down the aisle by ushers did not seem the best

113

way of attracting Bill's attention before asking a favour of him!

Lee turned and pushed his way through, swimming against a great tide of people, until he was once more safely outside.

There was nothing else to be done, he would just have to wait, patiently, until the conference was over.

The hours between two and five seemed to drag by, but at around half-past four a knot of women and men, armed with cameras or notebooks, began to form a dense semicircle round the Stage Door, elbowing him further and further back from it.

At ten to five a tall, burly policeman appeared and stood immediately to one side of the Stage Door exit.

Lee made his way to the opposite side of the group, using the reporters and photographers as cover.

At two minutes to five he heard a burst of applause from inside the hall and some of the audience swept by him.

It was two minutes past five when the Stage Door swung open and people began to emerge. Some were stopped briefly by reporters and questioned, odd ones photographed but many ignored, except by Lee.

He carefully scrutinized every face. Though it was less than a week since he'd last seen Bill, he no longer trusted himself to recognise him amongst this great crush of people. Indeed, several men with blond hair came out and Lee felt his heart jump, only to subside with disappointment as they didn't turn out to be Bill at all.

Lee, convinced that at least a hundred people had already left, was starting to panic. What if Bill had decided to avoid the press by using a separate exit?

When he'd almost given up hope, Lee caught sight of Bill coming out carrying a suitcase. He needn't have worried about not recognising him. There was no mistaking Bill's shock of hair and the bright blue eyes which flashed at a dark, bearded man with whom he was deep in conversation.

'Bill!' Lee shouted at the top of his voice.

But his shouts were drowned by the barrage of questions from the reporters and the scuffling of photographers as they battled for the best angle.

As Lee bobbed about like a helpless cork on a violent sea, trying to push his way through to Bill, the reporters aimed question after question.

'What was your impression of the Gulf during your visit?'

'Is the United States intervention likely to be stepped up?'

'Was there any agreement with the EEC over oil quotas?'

Frantically, Lee prised his way through the heaving bodies but each time he seemed to be making some headway, it was only to be thrust back again.

This had gone on for several minutes when he heard Bill's voice rise above the others. 'I'm sorry, ladies and gentlemen, I *have* to go! I have a plane to catch.'

Lee redoubled his efforts but, as Bill used the suitcase as a lever and the sea of people pushed back to let Bill through, they pushed Lee back with them.

He raced down to the end of the line where he could see a car waiting. He ducked down and risked getting his fingers stamped on as he crawled along the pavement, pushing his way through the forest of legs.

Just as Lee was getting up from his knees, he heard Bill saying, 'That's all, folks!'

'Bill!' he screamed.

But Bill didn't hear or see him.

The door slammed and the car drove away.

Lee and a number of photographers, who were still not content with the shots they'd got, ran after the car until it accelerated and left them, breathless, and in Lee's case sobbing with anger.

The crowd of reporters began to evaporate more quickly than it had grown, bumping into Lee in their efforts to leave.

A woman in a black suit noticed the tears streaming down Lee's face. 'What's up with you?'

'I *had* to talk to him!' Lee replied fiercely.

'Who, Senator Keever?'

'I have been trying to get to see him for days.' Lee's sobs which were mainly from frustration began to subside. 'I got *that* close and then you all got in the way!' he shouted at perplexed reporters as they rushed back to file their stories.

'You might still catch him, if you get a move on instead of blaming us,' the woman said.

'How?'

'Follow him to Heathrow Airport, that's where he's gone.'

'How do I get there?'

'Use the Underground. There's a station quite near. Go down the back of the Albert Hall, join the main road and keep going. The station's on your right.'

She'd hardly finished speaking before Lee had turned and was running through the crowd. Then a thought flashed across her mind. 'Hey, kid, aren't you ... ?' but before she could remember the name of the boy whose photograph had appeared on the front page of the paper she worked for, he was gone.

'George,' she said, stopping a photographer, 'does that kid I was talking to remind you of anyone?'

George looked baffled. 'No, should he?'

'Never mind, it's probably my imagination, let's get back to the office.'

Lee raced down Exhibition Road, trying to catch up with Bill Keever far faster than he had run away from him on the day they had met after their tennis match. Then he had been running away from thoughts of Chi. Now he felt he was running towards her.

When his path was blocked by a group of children larking about after their visit to the Science Museum, Lee leapt out into the gutter and kept running against the oncoming traffic, dodging cyclists.

A man crossing the road caught Lee's ankle with his umbrella and sent Lee sprawling in the gutter, but before the man could apologise Lee was up again and running.

Lee didn't even notice his hand was bleeding until he reached South Kensington Underground station and was slipping the coins into the machine for his ticket to Heathrow.

He made no mistake in reading the map, or finding the correct platform. Nor did he have to change trains, the first train to pull in was going all the way to Heathrow Airport.

Once on the train he only took his eyes off the narrow map above the window to check off each station as they arrived.

He blinked as the train emerged into the daylight after Earl's Court. Above ground the train seemed to travel more slowly. He checked his watch, it was ten to six. But he held his peace and just kept checking off the stations one by one.

Only one thing bothered him. On the map there appeared to be more than one Heathrow Station; the first served Terminals 1, 2 and 3 while the second was only for Terminal 4.

Forty-five minutes after he'd boarded the train Lee jumped off at the station which served the most terminals and, as he pounded up the escalator, saw a screen of departures that listed a flight to San Francisco which was already boarding in Terminal 3.

His mind was crystal clear as he raced through the airport. He didn't miss his way once and didn't stop until he got to the customs gate.

'Your boarding card?' the man said.

'I don't have one, I want to talk to somebody on the flight.'

The man shook his head. 'Sorry, you can't go through.'

'But I have to!'

'I'm sorry.'

Everything drained out of Lee. He had no more energy or emotion left. He walked slowly to the glass window of the spectators' lounge. Twenty minutes later he watched a Pan Am jet climbing into the sky and knew, finally, he had failed.

When the plane disappeared into the cloud, Lee walked up to the first policeman he could find and said, 'I am Lee Nguyen.'

TWELVE

'Soon be there now,' the policeman said without taking his eyes from the motorway.

'I am not in a hurry,' Lee muttered. He sat gloomily in the back of the police car, watching the countryside speeding past. He had spent the night in an unlocked police cell lying awake listening to the singing of a drunk in the next cell.

He had barely spoken since he'd given himself up to the police at Heathrow. Though he'd answered most of their questions, he had given only brief details about his journey. He'd left out Scotty altogether, not wishing to admit his mistake.

The police had assumed, as he offered no other explanation, that he had left the camp merely out of boredom. They gave him a mild telling off, for all the trouble and upset he'd caused both to his parents and the police, but beyond that they were very kind. They even sent out to a Chinese takeaway for food for him! He offered to pay, he still had ten of his twenty pounds left, but they refused.

Throughout it all, Lee sat perfectly still in a state of total numbness. It was almost as if he didn't dare to allow himself to feel anything for fear of unlocking such an enormous tidal wave of emotion that he would be in danger of being swept away by it.

To remain in this unnaturally calm state he blanked off the whole of his mind. There were no more thoughts of Bill or Chi and when the police offered him the chance to talk to his parents on the telephone he'd quietly refused.

Instead he concentrated fiercely on objects around him. His fingers gently traced the sharp, corrugated edges of the food container and though he didn't understand it, he read and memorized every word of a poster on the interview-room wall explaining the dangers of rabies.

He was helped by the practical attitude of the police, whose main concern was not to lose him again and to return him to his family as quickly as possible.

The invisible barrier he had set up was almost breached by a particularly kind policewoman. Noticing that he was very quiet, she asked if he was all right. Lee thought her parents must have been Indian. She had liquid, dark brown eyes and softly-permed black hair that curved round her face like feathers. Lee knew it was a mistake to look into her eyes. He almost cracked, but he looked away sharply and nodded and was relieved when she went off duty without another word.

The following day he offered to travel back by train, if they would lend him the money, but they'd refused. 'We just want to be sure you get back safely,' they replied, implying he might make a break for it, but Lee knew he wouldn't, there was nowhere left for him to run to.

During the long journey up the motorway he had almost wished the driver was chattier and he was forced to count phone boxes to blot out the disturbing memories of travelling more hopefully in the opposite direction. There were the roadworks he remembered going through with Erica and, when they turned off the motorway, there was the spot where he'd been picked up by Scotty.

The driver from London delivered him to the local police station and immediately left on the return journey. A younger, far more talkative officer, with hair almost as bright as Red's, got up to run him back to the camp.

'I've rung the director of the camp to say you're on your way.'

A sudden thought occurred to Lee. 'Please, can we go to the antique shop on the way?'

'I'm not a taxi service, you know!'

'I promise I will be very quick.'

When the car pulled up in front of the bow-fronted shop the policeman, in case Lee decided to make a dash for it, got out and walked towards the door with Lee.

The old woman, who'd been peering through the window, on seeing the car, the policeman and Lee together, flung open the door. The bell still clattered above her head as she shouted, 'That's the one! You've caught him at last!'

The policeman looked totally baffled by the woman's

outburst and Lee was forced to explain. 'I came into the shop last Tuesday and she reported me to the police because she thought I was trying to steal a ring.' Lee produced a grubby ten-pound note from his jeans and offered it to the woman. 'You said it was ten pounds and I've come back to buy it.'

Instead of grabbing the money, as he'd expected, she shrank away from it as if it might burst into flames.

The policeman was growing impatient to be off. 'Is the ring still for sale?'

'Well … yes.'

'Then hand it over and take the lad's money!'

Lee, back in the car, was too busy admiring the gold ring and thinking that it was the one good thing to come out of this whole sorry mess, to notice that the shopkeeper was still standing on the steps of her shop and staring in disbelief at the ten-pound note in her hand.

'You mustn't take it personally, son, she accuses everybody who goes in there of trying to rob her,' the policeman said with a laugh. 'As you can imagine, she doesn't sell very much!'

Back at the camp the director had conducted the entire interview with a hurt expression on his face, both his leather-patched elbows on the desk and fingertips meeting in a point below his thin lips as if he were praying.

'Is there something about the camp which you dislike, Lee? I welcomed you here and I had hoped you would come to see me if you had any problems. By running away, you make me feel I have failed you in some way.'

Lee was spared from having to answer this statement by the director's secretary popping her head round the door to say there was an urgent call waiting for him.

'Maybe we can have a proper chat later,' the director said. 'Meanwhile, your parents are waiting for you in your quarters.'

Lee walked slowly across the grass towards C Block, deliberately avoiding the route past the tennis courts. Though he felt as if he had been away for years, depressingly little had changed. It was chilly and there were no people about, except for Phong jogging round the tarmac path.

Lee had hardly entered the corridor before Tam ran down the

corridor towards him. 'Lee, is it really you? Look, I found Suzie's leg and I've made her a new dress. Isn't she pretty?'

The doll's auburn hair had been washed and the new frock was bright yellow. Her half-closed eye appeared to be winking at Lee who smiled at his sister. 'Not half as pretty as you.'

Tam almost knocked him over as she leaped into his arms. 'Oh, Lee, I *have* missed you!'

His mother appeared in the doorway of his parents' room. 'Tam, there'll be time enough for that later. Lee, your father and grandmother are waiting to talk to you.'

This was the moment above all others Lee had been dreading. 'Is Father very angry?'

What reply she might have given was interrupted by his father's stern voice. 'Lee, we're waiting!'

His father was standing, hands behind him, with his back to the light so that Lee was unable to make out his expression. Grandmother sat on the bed and she certainly looked very serious.

'Lee, how could you do this to us?' his father asked quietly.

'I'm sorry, Father.'

'Our name in all the papers!' Knowing what a private person his father was Lee realised how uncomfortable that must have made him. 'Don't you realise, Lee, you could have totally ruined our chances in this country?'

'I didn't think of it that way.'

Grandmother, who had been screwing her face up, trying to catch what Lee was saying, burst out with, 'What's he saying? Why does the boy mumble?'

Lee cleared his throat and spoke louder. 'I said I was sorry ...'

'I was talking to your father!' she snapped.

Lee hung his head. 'Sorry.'

'What did he say? He's mumbling again. The boy must be punished for what he's done.'

'Yes, Mother.'

'There's no question about it,' the old lady said firmly, 'he should!'

'I was agreeing with you, Mother!' Father wiped a hand across his face in despair. Whilst as head of the family she had every right to be present, her constant interruptions prevented him from conducting the conversation his way.

She nudged him in the ribs. 'Get on with it then!'

Father sighed. There would be other chances to talk to Lee privately, but for now, if the conversation were not to turn into a farce, he must end it quickly. 'You are confined to your room, except for study and meals, for the whole of next week.'

'Yes, Father,' Lee said meekly but he almost jumped out of his skin as a hand banged on the partition wall.

'Tell him the news!' his mother shouted.

'What news?' Lee asked.

'I don't think this is the moment,' Father called back rather primly.

'Nonsense!' Mother said as she bustled into the room and put her arms around Lee. 'After all, it is all thanks to Lee. My poor child, look at the state of your clothes!'

'What news?' Lee repeated.

Kim ran into the room, gave Lee a big, sloppy kiss and announced, 'We're all going to America!'

Lee sat down on the bed beside his grandmother. He couldn't believe what he'd just heard. 'Going where?'

'America,' his mother said, 'and it's all your doing, Lee!'

Lee's mouth dropped open. 'Mine? How?'

'Because you're so good at tennis, Lee!' Kim laughed.

'I think you're all mad and I don't know what any of you are talking about. Would one of you please explain?'

Lee's father moved forward. 'You remember Nancy's father, Bill Keever?'

'Only too well!'

'It seems he's a very good player, an ex-professional who played at Wimbledon for several years and he's still crazy about the game.'

'I know all that, but you told me off for beating him in our match.'

'It seems I was wrong about that,' father admitted. 'He thought you were such an exceptionally promising player that he's arranged a tennis scholarship for you at one of America's biggest colleges. He's even providing you with a coach!'

Lee looked from one to the other. 'This has to be a joke. You're teasing me, aren't you?'

His mother sat on the bed beside him and slipped an arm round Lee's shoulder. 'No, Lee, it's all true, every word.'

Lee's brain raced as he tried to come to terms with the idea. He almost laughed when he realised his struggles to get to talk to Bill Keever had been pointless! 'But how has Senator Keever done all this?'

'You never said he was a Senator before!' Father said sharply.

'I must have forgotten to mention it,' Lee said quickly.

'Well, it isn't all finalized yet, but he's pulling strings in the Immigration Department to speed things up and he's definitely going to sponsor us.'

Lee's mouth had opened like a stranded fish. 'But he lives in San Francisco.'

'Exactly where we're going,' his mother said with a broad smile.

Lee exploded. 'Then I'll see Chi!'

Everyone laughed as Lee blushed.

'I should think so, we've written to the Duongs and I wouldn't be at all surprised if they meet us at the airport.'

Everybody began talking at once but then, one by one, they drifted away and Lee was once more alone with his father and grandmother.

The old lady looked very serious as she spoke to her son. 'Lee does understand his punishment, doesn't he?'

Father hid his smile. 'Yes, I think so, Mother.'

Then Lee remembered. 'Grandmother, I've brought something for you.' He knelt down in front of her, opened her thin hand and placed the gold ring in her palm.

For a long time, with tears in her eyes, she gazed at it. Carefully, Lee picked the ring up and slipped it on to her finger. It was a perfect fit.

The old lady, tears trickling down her cheeks, threw her arms around Lee and drew him towards her. 'Maybe,' she said quietly, 'he shouldn't really be punished after all.'

Lee's father smiled. 'No, Mother, I think you're probably right, as usual.'

Three months later, Lee was hopping about with impatience beside the minibus, anxious to be off to the airport, but the rest of the family kept disappearing, anxious to have 'one last word' with somebody, despite the huge send-off party they'd had which had gone on until the small hours.

Eventually it was Nancy who put her foot down. 'If you're not all in the bus soon you won't need to say goodbye, you'll miss the flight!'

They all helped Grandmother up the steps and piled in after her. As the bus drove along the front of the administration block and everyone waved, Lee took a last look back at the camp which he'd thought he'd never be leaving for good.

As the striped pole lifted Nancy, who was driving, paused before turning out into the main road for a taxi to turn into the camp.

Father leaped out of his seat and opened the minibus door. 'Loc! It's Loc!'

The thin, smiling man climbed out of the taxi and the two brothers hugged. Soon everyone, except Nancy and the bewildered taxi driver, was dancing and shouting at Uncle Loc.

Nancy leaned out of the window. 'We have to go or you'll miss the plane!'

'But it's all different now,' Father said and Lee thought his heart was going to stop beating. 'This is my brother Loc, whom we've been trying to get out of Hong Kong for so long. It's four years since we met and we can't possibly go now.'

To Lee's enormous relief, Nancy was very firm. 'Why doesn't Loc come with us to the airport and you can discuss it on the way?'

They all helped Grandmother back into the bus and Nancy was about to slip the engine into gear when the taxi driver, upset at seeing his passenger being hijacked, appeared at her window. 'And what about my fare?'

Nancy gave him a ten-pound note saying, 'Keep the change!' and drove off.

'Thanks a lot, lady,' the taxi driver said to himself. It was a long while since anybody had given him a ten p tip!

Lee's father and Loc argued all the way to the airport and

several times Lee felt his heart sinking, but in the end Loc insisted. 'Look, I've managed to follow you this far, what makes you think I won't make it to America?'

Even so, Lee didn't relax until they were on the plane and it was taxiing down the runway.

As it flew high above the English countryside Lee remembered his long journey. He had never thought of it as wasted, more as an offering to the gods. He had never really explained to his parents why he'd run away from the camp, only Chi knew the whole story. How strange their going to America might never have happened but for his ability to repair cars and his skill in tennis, both of which his father had always despised.

But for Lee, looking back, the most important part of his journey was that in those few days he had got a far better impression of England than he had throughout the two years in the camp and he knew he would never forget the kindness shown to him by people like Scotty, Erica and poor old Red.

During the long flight he had cause to remember Erica's encouraging words about his relationship with Chi because the closer they drew to America, the more Lee began to get cold feet. For three whole years the idea of being reunited with Chi had been the core, the driving force behind his whole life. Now it was almost a reality, he was forced to wonder if he might have blown up their relationship out of all proportion.

'Look!' Tam pointed excitedly out of the window. 'There's the Golden Gate!'

Lee braced himself for a bumpy landing.

He was the last of the family to leave Immigration and walk out into the arrival lounge of the International Airport.

His mother was already hugging Minh Duong, who was carrying their baby son. Lee's father was shaking hands with Hue who looked very at home in a brightly-coloured beach shirt with palm trees on it. Tam was bobbing up and down alongside them and Kim was tickling the baby under the chin while Grandmother looked on.

Lee searched the lounge but could see no sign of Chi! Then he noticed a slim Vietnamese girl standing to one side of the Duongs. Though her trousers were black they were not the traditional, baggy type but stylishly cut silk ones. She wore them with low-heeled shoes and a flowing lilac smock.

But the most striking feature was her hair. Cut very short, it emphasised not only the curve of her cheekbones, but her enormous eyes, eyes which glowed at Lee.

Lee dropped his case and ran towards her, falling into her outstretched arms.

'I hardly recognised you, you've changed so much!' he whispered into her hair which smelled faintly of almond blossom.

'Not inside, I haven't.'

'Nor me, but I was so frightened about meeting you again.'

'Me too,' she said, 'but I always told you we would be together one day. Now I know everything is going to be all right.'

They kissed and clung to each other for a long time before, hand in hand behind their parents, they left the airport.

Grandmother kept saying, loudly, 'She seems a very forward young girl.'

But nobody heard her.

A Selected List of Fiction from Mammoth

While every effort is made to keep prices low, it is sometimes necessary to increase prices at short notice. Mandarin Paperbacks reserves the right to show new retail prices on covers which may differ from those previously advertised in the text or elsewhere.

The prices shown below were correct at the time of going to press.